REECE

Susan Fisher-Davis

Men of Clifton, Montana

Book 11

Erotic Romance

Reece Men of Clifton, Montana Book 11
Copyright © 2020 Susan Fisher-Davis
First print publication: September 2020
ISBN: 9798689290980
Cover Photo: iStock.com
Cover design by Amy Valentini
All cover art copyright © 2020 by Susan Davis

PUBLISHER: Blue Whiskey Publishing
Susan Davis

Email: www.susanfisherdavisauthor.com

Newsletter: www.susanfisherdavisauthor.weebly.com/contact

Webpage: www.susanfisherdavisauthor.weebly.com

Acknowledgments

To my betas, Toby, Renee, Stacy, and Ginny—
you ladies are the best and I love all of you.

To my husband, Rob—you are my rock.

To Amy Valentini - The best editor an author
could have.
I'm honored to call you my friend.

To the ladies in my Facebook group: Susan's
Hot Cowboys—you make it fun.

As always to you, my readers,
I wouldn't be able to do this without you.
I love each and every one of you and I
appreciate your support.
Thank you.

Chapter One

Life was changing for Darissa Gates, yet it wasn't. She'd moved to Clifton, Montana to be close to her family but still felt something was missing. It wasn't that she didn't enjoy being with her family, she did. She was helping at the diner owned by her aunt and uncle and seeing more of her sisters than she had in years. Since she wasn't working today, she wasn't sure what she was going to do but sitting alone in the apartment would just let her mind wander back to that amazing night she couldn't seem to forget.

After deciding to get out, she walked along the sidewalk past the shops and smiled when she saw the snow flurries. Some people just hated snow but she, along with her sisters, loved it. Having been born and raised in New Mexico, they never saw snow unless it was in pictures or on TV and in movies. Any chance to see it for real and be out in it really appealed to her.

She entered a store just to have something to do. Moving around the store, she stopped when she heard someone say her name, and glanced over to see Kenzie Worthington walking to her. Kenzie was a beautiful woman with wheat-colored hair. She had beautiful blue eyes. She was taller than her, standing at five-six. Kenzie was a wills, trusts, and estates attorney in Dirk Wallace's office. Although the woman had a gorgeous smile, it never seemed to reach the sadness in her eyes. One day, she'd like to know why her friend was so sad. Probably over a man. She wondered if Kenzie was still upset over her divorce.

"Hi, Kenzie. How are you?"

"I'm good, Rissa. How about you?" Everyone in Clifton called her Rissa because that was how her family had introduced her. She liked it. It was familiar.

"Same. I'm off today so I decided to do some shopping, although I haven't bought a thing," she said with a laugh.

"I know what you mean. I just had lunch and had a few minutes to kill so I thought I'd stop in here."

Rissa smiled. *Here* was Paige's, and Paige's was a lingerie shop. It sold some racy and sexy clothing.

"I love the lingerie here, but not having a man to wear it for seems like I'm wasting my time." Rissa shook her head.

"I know. But I love it so much. I buy it just for me. Not a man. Not anymore." Kenzie smiled.

"That's true. Why should it be just for them?"

"With a man, you only need it in case of a fire but for me, I know I'm wearing something sexy under my clothes."

Rissa laughed. "In case of a fire. I love that. We'd have to have something to throw on, wouldn't we? Yeah, I do have some sexy stuff too. I used to wear it for Nolan, but he couldn't care less. So, you're right, I'm going to buy some for me."

"Go for it." Kenzie looked at the watch on her wrist. "I have to get back to the office. I'll talk to you soon, Rissa."

"Sure. Hey, I'd love to get together sometime."

"Sounds fun. We'll talk soon." Kenzie gave a wave then walked out.

Rissa waved to her. She knew something or someone had hurt Kenzie and she wanted to know what or who it was. Kenzie was so beautiful, and she deserved to be happy. Maybe Rissa was wrong about her having a sense of sadness about her, but she didn't think so.

After deciding to buy a few new bras and panties, she headed home.

Later, as she sat on the sofa, she picked up the remote and aimed it at the TV to see a Valentine's Day movie was on, even though it was still two weeks away. Although it wasn't far off, it did her no good. There was no man in her life anymore. When Nolan had been around, he never did anything with her on that day. He always made reservations for a few days later. Too crowded, he'd say. She hadn't cared if it was wall to wall people, she wanted to go out on that day. A lot of couples did, so why couldn't they?

"What an egotistical jerk," she murmured as she pulled the quilt off the back of the couch and covered herself with it.

Shaking her head, she couldn't believe she'd been so stupid where he was concerned. She was glad she decided to get away from him because who knew how much worse it could have gotten. Telling her sisters about it had been so hard, but their support meant the world to her. They would never look down on her no matter what she'd done. Nolan had been good to her at the beginning of their relationship but then he got possessive and she didn't feel like she even belonged to herself. He had started to frighten her, so much so she decided she needed to leave him and come to Clifton. Only he followed her, and now she lived in fear of what he might do.

A knock at her door startled her. Aiming the remote at the TV, Rissa muted it, threw the quilt off, then pushed herself up from the sofa to make her way to the door. She blew out a relieved breath when she heard Lanie's voice come through the door.

"Come on, Rissa. Deidra and I are freezing out here," she yelled.

Rissa flipped the outside light on, opened the door, and her sisters came in, bringing the cold with them. Snow peppered the shoulders of their coats and the beanies on their heads. She looked out to see snow coming down slow and steady, so it coated the steps that led to the ground. She quickly closed the door, locked it, and turned to watch her sisters as they took off their beanies, gloves, and coats then hung them on the coat rack beside the door. They headed for the couch and flopped down on it. She grinned then sat down between them and tugged the large quilt over them.

"What are you two doing out in this weather?"

"We were shopping for Valentine's Day gifts. It's just two weeks away, ya know. We were heading home when we decided to stop in and see you for a few minutes," Deidra said with a smile.

"Did you find anything?"

Lanie and Deidra laughed.

"We decided that both Trent and Preston would rather see us in lingerie than us buying them gifts. So, we went to Paige's. We figured the men would love it," Lanie said.

"Yeah, they will. I was in Paige's today and bought some new bras and panties." Rissa frowned.

"What's wrong, Rissa?" Deidra asked her while rubbing her arm.

"Nothing." She blew out a breath. "Everything. I hate it that I don't have a man anymore."

"Anymore? Girl, you never had a man. You had a spoiled brat for a boyfriend." Lanie folded her arms and glared at her.

"I know, but you two are so happy, and I want that too, so much."

"You'll find it one day." Deidra grabbed her hand.

"I thought I'd found him—"

"I just said he wasn't a man," Lanie snapped.

"I'm not talking about Nolan. Remember when I broke it off with him back in August?"

"Smartest thing you did...at the time...then you took him back." Deidra scowled.

Rissa leaned her head back and closed her eyes. At that moment, the memory of that night with *him* filled her mind. Every detail was as clear as if it was happening now.

Standing in the lobby of the hotel, Rissa watched the numbers above the elevator count down until the doors whooshed open. After stepping inside, she turned and pressed the number six for her floor, relaxed, and watched the doors begin to close. Suddenly, a hand reached inside, stopping them. The doors slid open again, and a gorgeous cowboy stepped inside the car. He pressed the number seven, then stepped to the back, leaned against the wall, looked over at her, and put his fingers to the brim of his hat. He gave her a nod, then hooked his thumbs on the front pockets of his jeans.

She almost swallowed her gum when he had looked at her and butterflies took flight in her belly. Taking a deep breath, she smiled then looked up to watch the numbers change as the elevator ascended. The scent of his aftershave made her inhale deeply, and she couldn't help but glance over at him. He was very tall, even leaning against the wall, she could see he had long legs. Her eyes ran up from his distressed cowboy boots, jean-clad legs to his fly, and she almost groaned as she saw the way it cupped his sex. This man was simply the hottest thing she'd ever seen, and being a barrel racer, she'd seen a lot of sexy cowboys.

She turned, folded her arms, leaned against the wall, and faced him. His red T-shirt hugged a flat stomach and incredible looking pecs. The sleeves stretched tight around his biceps and she could see the muscles flexing in his arms. The thick, dark hair on his forearms had her clenching her fists to keep from running her fingers through it. Slowly, she raised her eyes to his neck, and although he was clean-shaven, she could see a faint shadow there, on his strong jaw, and lower face, and it surrounded the most delicious pair of lips she'd ever seen on a man. Her eyes moved up to his straight nose then to his eyes, which were watching her. Their eyes met and held, and his were gorgeous. His eyelashes were thick and lush, making her pissed that a man should have such lashes. His eyes were dark yet cool at the same time, rimmed in a stormy, nearly black ring at the edges, then brightened to a lighter blue toward the center like a deep lagoon with its center lit by sunshine. She'd never seen eyes like his, and they were so gorgeous in his tanned face. There were fine lines at the corners of his eyes, and the black hair curling on the nape of his neck looked so silky. Clearing her throat, she turned her gaze on to watch the numbers when the elevator stopped. They had reached the third floor already. The doors opened, and two young women stepped inside. They looked at her but immediately dismissed her when their eyes locked on the cowboy. They both moved to stand beside him.

"Hi," one of them said.

"Ma'am," he said in a deep voice as he touched the brim of his hat.

"Are you in town for the rodeo?" the other one asked as she moved closer to him.

"Yes, ma'am."

"Are you competing in it?"

Rissa watched as the young woman who asked the question leaned against the wall beside him and put her hands behind her back to push her breasts out. The girl was as subtle as a freight train. She pulled her bottom lip between her teeth to hold back a grin. The cowboy seemed a little uncomfortable.

"Just a spectator."

"Are you here alone?" one asked and glanced over to her.

Rissa looked at him to see him looking at her. Then he looked back to the young woman.

"I'm here alone," he said.

"Awesome! Would you like to get together for a drink? You could come up to our room. We can't go into the bar."

Awesome? She had trouble not laughing as she watched the cowboy straighten up, fold his arms across his broad chest, and look at the two young women.

"You can't go into the bar? Why is that?" The smirk and raised eyebrow gave it away that he knew precisely why they couldn't.

"We're not quite twenty-one."

"Quite twenty-one? Either you're not twenty-one, or you are. There's no *quite* about it, and seeing as that would be illegal, that's one reason I'll have to pass."

"One reason? What's another one?"

"I'm thirty-six, and you're way too young for me."

The elevator stopped on the fourth floor, and the girls stepped out then waved at him as they giggled.

"If you change your mind, we're in four twenty, and there are two other friends of ours here, on the second floor."

The doors slid closed, and she heard the cowboy blow out a breath as he leaned against the wall and hooked his thumbs into the front pockets of his jeans again. They rode in silence to her floor. The doors slid open, and she stepped out, but before she started toward her room, his voice stopped her.

"Now if *you* want to get a drink in the bar downstairs, darlin', I'll be there around six."

She turned to look at him and smiled.

"Awesome," she said, then imitated the girls by waving and giggling at him.

His lips rose in a slow, sexy grin, and she was sure her knees were going to give out, then the doors slid closed.

She hemmed and hawed about meeting him in the bar. After all, she didn't know him from Adam, but boy, did she want to. He was simply scrumptious, and she wanted to do all kinds of things to him and let him do the same to her. She finally decided to go for it and pulled on a green summer dress that matched her eyes. The square neckline showed the tops of her breasts, and wedge sandals covered her feet. Even with four-inch heels on, being only five foot one, her cowboy was going to tower over her. *God!* She loved tall men. Her red toenails peeked out the open toes of her shoes.

Taking a deep breath, she picked up her purse and keycard, then left her room to head for the elevator. It was five minutes to six. She didn't want to get there too early and seem anxious. Placing a hand over her belly, she tried to calm herself then pushed the button for the elevator. When the doors slid open, she hesitated but then stepped inside. Glancing down at the top of her breasts, she wondered if she should wear something like this? Would he think she was trying to entice him? Of course, she was hoping she would. She wanted to do something she'd never done before and if all went well, she hoped to end up in his room for the night. If she got any type of bad vibe, she'd be out of there in a heartbeat. *You never had one about Nolan and look how that turned out.*

"Yeah, he certainly fooled me," she muttered.

The elevator came to a stop, and the doors slid open. Sucking in a deep breath, Rissa stepped into the lobby and headed in the direction of the bar. Men turned their heads to watch her as she crossed the lobby. She had let her long dark hair down around her shoulders, and her makeup was perfect. Cowboys tipped their hats at her as they passed. At the entrance to the bar, she stopped and looked inside. It was just bright enough to see everyone, and she looked around for him but didn't see him. Had he changed his mind? Disappointment shot through her, but maybe it was fate that he hadn't shown. She'd never done anything like this before and now the gods were telling her to turn around and leave.

What are you thinking? She chastised herself for even thinking of doing something like this. It was for the best. She sucked in a breath and exhaled, then decided to have a drink to calm herself. She was disappointed yet relieved at the same time.

"I thought maybe you weren't going to show, sweetheart," a deep voice said next to her ear, making her shiver.

Turning, she looked up at him and smiled. "I needed a drink."

He chuckled, and she wanted to ride him right there. He jerked his chin for her to go in and when he placed his hand on the small of her back, she bit her lip to hold back a moan.

Just that small touch had her wanting to tell him that she didn't need a drink, she just needed him, but he led her to a table. He held the chair for her, moved around the table and took a seat, and stared at her. The heat poured into her cheeks. No man had ever looked at her the way he did. Fate. It was fate that he *had* shown. *And you were just telling yourself to go!*

"But what would one drink hurt?" she mumbled.

"What?" he asked.

"Nothing. Just talking to myself."

"You are breathtakingly beautiful," he murmured.

"Thank you. I'm D—" She held her hand out but stopped talking when he held his hand up.

"No names. We both know what this is about. One night. If that's a problem, maybe you should leave now."

She stared at him and realized now was her chance. Her chance to back out, but then lifted her lips in a slow smile. "I'm not going anywhere. Are you?"

"Only to my room with you." He grinned at her.

His grin was deadly, and if he could make her hot with just that, imagine what he could do with those lips that surrounded it. She did want to find out.

"Sounds good to me, cowboy."

Giving her a nod, he raised his hand to signal to a waitress who came over to them.

"What would you like to drink, darlin'?"

"Callahan Whiskey on the rocks."

"I'm impressed. Damn fine whiskey." He looked up at the waitress. "I'll have the same."

She noticed the waitress stared at him, winked, and walked off. It was clear she had no problem flirting with him in front of her. Rissa laughed softly.

"What?" he asked her.

"I guess you have women coming on to you all the time."

He shrugged. "Some. I like to do the chasing though. Some women are just too brazen for me."

"You're not married, are you?"

"I wouldn't be here with you if I was. Besides, I'm not the settling down type. Are you married?"

"I wouldn't be here with you if I was," she repeated his words with a smile.

Suddenly, not knowing what else to say she glanced around the bar. It was crowded but seemed like a nice place. The lights were low but not to the point that she couldn't see. A stage sat against a back wall and she wondered if a band would play. Music was playing through speakers but low enough not to disturb the patrons. People filled the long bar at the back wall, laughter and conversations could be heard.

The waitress brought their drinks and set them down in front of them. She seemed to hesitate beside the table, but when the cowboy didn't look up at her, she huffed and walked off. Rissa lifted her glass and took a sip. She loved whiskey. Her aunt had sent her a bottle of Callahan Whiskey for Christmas one year, and she fell in love with it. She'd later found out that the whiskey was made in Spring City, Montana, another small town next to Clifton where her aunt lived. She set her glass down and glanced around again. When she turned to look at him again, his gaze was on the top of her breasts then he raised his eyes slowly to stare into hers. He made her hot with just a look.

"I'm finished with my drink," she whispered.

He shot to his feet, laid money on the table then helped her up, took her hand, and led her from the bar and into the lobby. It took a few minutes for her eyes to adjust to the brightness after being in the bar, but it didn't seem to bother him as he pulled her behind him to the elevator.

They stood in front of it but didn't say a word. When the doors slid open, they stepped inside. He put his hands on her arms and moved her to one side of the elevator then he moved to the opposite wall. She raised an eyebrow at him.

"If I touch you now, we'll never get out of this elevator," he murmured.

She hissed in a breath, but she knew what he meant. She couldn't wait to run her hands and mouth all over this gorgeous man, but she knew he was right. They needed to get to his room first. The elevator came to a halt, and the doors opened. She looked over at him to see him staring at her.

"Not too late to back out, darlin'."

With a smile, she pushed away from the wall, stepped out of the elevator then turned to look at him. He grinned, stepped out beside her then took her hand in his and led her down the hallway then stopped at a door. He reached into the back pocket of his jeans, pulled his wallet out then removed the room keycard. After he inserted it, he pushed the door open and held it for her.

Taking a deep breath, she hesitated then entered the room with him behind her. She heard him lock the door then she turned to look at him to see him leaning back against it with his arms folded, staring at her. Swallowing hard, she wondered what in the hell she was doing. As she watched, a slow grin lifted his lips, and when he took his bottom lip between his teeth, she almost attacked him.

"Thinking about it, aren't you?"

"I've never done this before," she whispered.

He pushed off from the door and sauntered to her. Stopping in front of her, he placed his finger under her chin and tilted her face up.

"And you don't have to do it now. I'll walk you to your room, and we can forget we ever met. But I have to tell ya, darlin', I've never wanted a woman more. But if you want to leave, I won't stop you. I've never forced a woman in my life, and I don't intend to start with you."

She stared up at him, and she could see the truth in his eyes. Hell, he would never have to force a woman. She smiled and placed her hands on his hard chest.

"Then what are you waiting for, cowboy?" She reached up, removed his cowboy hat, tossed it aside, then combed her fingers through his thick dark hair.

His lips slammed down on hers, forcing her mouth open, making her moan as his tongue slid into her mouth. She tangled hers with his. Damn, he could kiss. He slowly lifted his mouth from hers, then led her into a bedroom. She could see the large bathroom through a doorway. *So, this is what a suite is like.*

When he lifted her and set her on the dresser, she was sure she had an orgasm when he spread her legs and stepped between them. He pressed his lips to hers and never removed his mouth as he ran his hands down her waist to her legs. His hands moved slowly, oh so slowly, up her thighs under her dress to the waistband of her panties. He hooked his fingers in them and pulled them down. Placing her palms on the dresser, she lifted her hips to help him. He tugged them down her legs and, pulled them off. His hands moved under her dress again, and he slid one finger along her slit. She moaned against his lips. He slowly raised his lips from hers and gazed into her eyes.

"You're wet, sweetheart. Have you been thinking about this?"

"Yes, ever since I saw you in the elevator."

He grinned against her lips. "Me too. You smell amazing, and I bet you taste even better."

He stuck his finger in his mouth, and she watched him suck her essence off. Then he placed his lips against hers again and kissed her hard and deep.

Rissa raked her fingers through his thick hair and grabbed fistfuls of it, trying to bring him closer. She pulled her lips from his and stared into those gorgeous eyes.

"Please, I need you now," she whispered.

"Not half as much as I need you." He reached behind him, and she watched as he retrieved a condom from his wallet, then placed it on the dresser beside her. She grabbed the condom then reached between them to place her hand over his hard cock straining against the fly of his jeans, making him groan. "If I don't have you soon, I'm going to go insane."

She unsnapped his jeans and lowered the zipper, then moved her hand inside to wrap her fingers around him. He was amazing. She squeezed him, and he hissed in a breath. Pushing his jeans and underwear down, she looked down to see his engorged cock jutting out. She'd never wanted a man more. She ripped open the condom, rolled it down over him, and he blew out a breath when it completely covered him. He grabbed her legs behind her knees and jerked her forward then took her lips in a deep kiss as he guided himself inside. He thrust hard, making her gasp. She wrapped her legs around him. He reached behind her and unzipped her dress, tugging the top down to bare her breasts since she wasn't wearing a bra.

"Dear God, you're perfect," he murmured as he dipped his head and placed his mouth over a nipple and sucked on it. His tongue swirled around it. Then he pulled at it with his teeth while he ran the pad of his thumb over the other one. Her nipples hardened and she wanted him to take her over. She needed that orgasm and she knew he could get her there.

She knew what he'd meant when he said he'd go insane. She was on fire and needed him to take her over the edge. She dug her nails into his hard ass.

"Please," she whimpered.

He raised his head and looked at her.

"I will, darlin'. I will." Then he began moving in and out of her, and she moved her hips in rhythm with his. He hooked his arms under her legs, behind her knees, opening her wider for him then began to pound hard into her. When his thumb touched her clitoris, she almost screamed, it was that intense.

"Take me over...God, please, now." She had never begged during sex in her life, but this man was driving her insane, and she needed that orgasm.

"Yes, ma'am," he said against her lips then slammed into her harder and moved his thumb against her.

"Oh, God! Yes!" She screamed when she came and put her face into the crook of his neck and bit him. *Bit him!* Dear Lord, she still wanted more. He grunted when she bit him but kept pounding into her.

"Let's go for another one, darlin'."

Another one? She was still coming down from the first one, and he wanted to go for another one? Just as that thought left her head, he continued to move his thumb against her clitoris, and she was so sensitive that it quickly threw her over again. Groaning, she pulled his hair.

"Kiss me," she whispered and sighed when his lips met hers in a long, slow kiss. She screamed in his mouth as another orgasm hit her hard, and a deep guttural groan tore from him as he came. She actually felt him throbbing inside her. He pumped a few more times, then stopped, lifted his lips from hers, and leaned his forehead against hers as they both tried to catch their breaths. Their eyes met, and they started laughing.

"Fuck, that was hot," he said.

"Yes. Can we do it again?" she said between deep breaths.

"Oh yeah, darlin'. You're not leaving this room until tomorrow morning. I said tonight, and we have a lot of night left. How about a shower?" He stepped back from her, pulled his jeans up, zipped them, but left them unsnapped. He picked up his wallet, walked to a door, opened it, then disappeared inside. She frowned and wondered what he was doing, but then he reentered the room.

"I'll be right back," he said then entered the bathroom, and she was sure it was to dispose of the condom. When he came back out, he leaned against the wall beside the dresser, folded his arms, and stared at her.

"Is that a closet?" she asked as she pointed to where he'd gone earlier. At his nod, she tilted her head. "What did you do in there?"

"I put my wallet in the safe that's in there. Doesn't your suite have a safe?"

"Uh, no. I don't have a *suite*. I have a *room*."

"I see. Do you plan on sitting there all night?"

"I'm not sure I can get down without falling. You made me weak in the knees." She was very serious since her feet dangled several inches off the floor as she still sat on the dresser.

That sexy grin lifted his lips as he pushed off the wall and moved to stand in front of her. He glanced down to her breasts, and she was amazed that she wasn't shy at being practically completely naked in front of him. He reached down to her foot, lifted it, and removed one shoe, then the other one. His touch made her tremble.

"I like these red toenails." He spread her legs, stepped between them, then picked her up and carried her into the bathroom where he set her on her feet and pushed her dress down off her hips, making it fall in a pool around her feet.

"I hope you have more condoms."

He laughed. "I'm always prepared. I never have sex without one. You're the only woman I've even thought about not wearing one with. I wanted skin on skin."

"That would be fantastic, but since we don't actually know each other..."

"Yes, ma'am." He turned from her, reached into the shower, and the room quickly filled with steam.

He tugged his T-shirt off over his head, and she had to bite her cheek so she wouldn't moan. His chest and stomach were terrific. His hard pecs, six-pack stomach, and belly button were covered with a light smattering of hair that disappeared into his jeans. That dark hair had her salivating. She watched as he sat on the edge of the tub and toed off his cowboy boots then stood and pushed his jeans down. *Boxer briefs.* Sexiest underwear a man could wear in her opinion. Then he pushed them down. *Oh, my.* To say he was hung would be a huge understatement. *Huge!* He pulled his socks off, then stood naked in front of her, and she wanted him again. When he cleared his throat, she looked up at him and smiled, then moved to where he stood. She got on her toes to kiss him. He started to deepen the kiss when his cellphone buzzed from in the room. He huffed.

"I have to get that. Get in the shower, and I'll join you in a minute. Don't wash. I want to do it."

She shivered as she thought of his hands running all over her again, and she was going to return the favor once he came back. She could hear him talking but not what he was saying. Shrugging, she stepped into the shower and waited for her cowboy...

"Rissa. Rissa," Lanie was saying her name and rubbing her arm.

She opened her eyes and looked at her sisters. With a deep inhalation, she blew out the air as if calming her body then told her sisters about that amazing night with a hot cowboy in Helena. Of course, she left out the fine details, but they got the gist. When she finished, she looked at them to see identical expressions of disbelief on their faces, and she couldn't stop the laughter from bubbling out.

"Are you serious?" Deidra sat up.

"Yep. It was the best sex I ever had, and I should have pushed for information about him, but I didn't and now I'll never find him again." She blinked tears from her eyes.

"So, you took Nolan back because you were feeling vulnerable and thinking you'd never see your cowboy again." Lanie rubbed her back.

"I won't see him again. Unless he suddenly comes through Clifton, there's a snowball's chance in hell that I'll ever see that man again. I wrote my number down and placed it on the dresser, but he didn't call me. I *was* feeling vulnerable and so I let Nolan talk me into going back to him. I know I shouldn't have." She shook her head.

"You'll find someone new, sis. There are a lot of gorgeous men in this town and Hartland and Spring City. I could name several of them you'd like. They're all hot. You might find one and fall in love just like we did." Lanie smiled.

"I hope so but I'm not going to hold my breath that any man will ever be as good as that cowboy. Once the weather clears though, I'm seriously going to look for a man of my own. I might not be able to find one who can rock my world like my cowboy did, but maybe one who could move it a little. Anyway, shouldn't you be heading home? The weather is getting worse. Unless you want to stay here?"

"The roads weren't bad yet...but yeah, we'd better get going. We just thought we'd stop in and check on you." Lanie stood, walked to the coat rack, pulled on her coat and beanie, and Deidra did the same then they both hugged Rissa as she stood beside them.

"Lock the door. We'll talk to you tomorrow," Deidra said as she hugged her tighter. "You will find someone," she whispered in her ear. "I can think of quite a few off the top of my head too."

Rissa nodded and hugged her then Lanie again, and they walked out the door to head down the steps.

"Please be careful walking down these metal steps and driving home. Call your men. They're probably worried."

"Doing it now," Lanie said as she held her cellphone up and walked down the stairs.

Rissa smiled as she watched her sisters make their way down. She frowned as she realized she needed to get some salt and sprinkle it on them before she, or someone else, falls on their ass while on the slick steps.

"Hey," she called out, making them both stop, turn around, and look up at her. "Could Preston or Trent pick up a bag of salt for the stairs?"

Lanie nodded. "I'll ask Trent to get some for you. He has to go to the feed store tomorrow if the weather is okay."

"Thanks, Lanie. I appreciate you both. Love you," she said, then closed the door. It was too damn cold to stay out there too long, but she loved it.

Locking the door behind her, she headed for the sofa again then flopped down. Too bad her sisters couldn't spend the night, but she knew they wanted to get home to their men and who could blame them. Preston and Trent were drop-dead gorgeous. She was happy for her sisters but seeing those sexy men they had made her even sadder knowing she'd never see her cowboy again. Too bad. He'd been so sexy and had made her feel so special. The sex had been so damn good, the best she'd ever had and probably ever will.

There wasn't anywhere on her that he hadn't known intimately by the end of that night, and she knew every inch of him too. How could two people have so much chemistry, so much heat, and then walk away never to see each other again? Damn. He had been tender when he'd needed to be, but when he took her against the wall, he demanded everything from her, and she had shocked herself that she gave as good as she got—even biting his neck again. Mentally groaning, she couldn't believe how hot it had been, and it made her heart ache that she'd probably never have that again with another man.

Why hadn't he called? He had to have seen her number, right? What if he hadn't? Well, too late now. She didn't know his name or where he was from. He'd told the girls in the elevator that he was just a spectator so he could be from anywhere. *Damn it!* She should have demanded his name or at least held out until she'd gotten it from him, and she knew she could have. With a deep sigh, she pulled the quilt over her and picked up the remote to look for something to watch.

A few days later, Rissa stood at the end of the counter at the diner with her chin propped in her hand as she spun her pen around on the counter with the other one, all the while popping her bubblegum. The place was empty, and she was sure it was because of the snow coming down heavily outside. She hated being bored. Blowing a bubble, she glanced at the door when the bell rang, quickly straightened up, inhaled, and swallowed her gum then hurried into the kitchen and peered out the window between the kitchen and the counter.

A customer took a seat at the counter and glanced around. There was no way she was going out there. Taking a deep breath, she scanned the kitchen, hoping her aunt, Lanie, or Deidra, would be here, but they had disappeared into the cooler to do inventory. *Oh, dear God! She could not go out there.*

It was *him.* She was sure of it. What was he doing here? Slowly making her way to the pass-through window, she peeked over the shelf and looked at him. It *was* him. There was no doubting it, she was sure. She knew every inch of that sexy body, and she saw his gorgeous face every night when she closed her eyes to sleep. She let out a squeal when someone touched her back, and she spun around to see Lanie standing behind her.

"You're awfully jumpy," Lanie said with a laugh.

"My cowboy is here," she whispered.

"In Clifton?"

"No. Here. In. The. Diner."

"Oh, my God! Seriously?" Lanie peered out the opening. "Where?"

"Sitting at the counter. He has a black cowboy hat on." She peered out again.

Lanie moved her aside and looked out then shook her head.

"I only see Reece."

Rissa had heard that name mentioned many times. She stood on her toes and looked. "I've never met Reece, but my *cowboy* is right there," she said through clenched teeth while pointing to the counter.

"I'm going to get Reece some coffee, and I'll look around. Maybe he moved to a booth, although I don't know why anyone is out in this weather. I'll be glad when Trent gets here to take me home."

Rissa nodded as she watched Lanie leave the kitchen then she peeked out to see her walking to *him* and pouring him a cup of coffee. She watched Lanie glance around then head back to the kitchen.

"I don't see anyone else." Lanie stared at her.

"You just poured him a cup of coffee," she snapped.

"I poured Reece a cup of coffee—" Lanie gasped. "Oh my God! Reece is your cowboy."

"What?"

"Reece Maddox is who I just poured a cup of coffee for."

"Reece, Preston's friend, he's...my cowboy?" She had to sit down because the room was swaying.

Lanie grabbed her arm and led her to a stool. "Sit down before you fall."

"Yes—" She groaned and placed her hands over her face. "What are the odds?"

"I have no idea."

"No idea about what?" Deidra asked as she entered the kitchen then reached for her coat.

"Reece is Rissa's cowboy," Lanie told her.

"What are you talking about?" Deidra asked her with a frown.

"Reece is the man Rissa had the hot night with in Helena," Lanie whispered.

Deidra stared at them then burst out laughing. Rissa swatted at her, but Deidra continued to laugh. She wiped tears from her eyes.

"This is too funny."

"It is not funny," Rissa growled. "Well, that's just great. I'm going home. I refuse to go out there." She hopped down and began to pull on her coat.

"So, you're just going to stop working? You have to face him sometime, and just think, you found your sexy cowboy after all. Maybe you can take up where you left off," Lanie said, smiling.

Rissa hesitated and nibbled on her bottom lip. Should she? *No!* He'd made it clear how he felt when he never called her. She'd left her number for him, and he made the decision to keep it a one-night stand. Clenching her hands into fists, her nails dug into her palms. She took a deep breath and looked at Deidra, then Lanie.

"No. He never called, so he has no desire to take up where we left off. I'll work a double for you tomorrow, Lanie, but I will not go out there right now."

"Oh, you will because I'm not waiting on him. Trent just came in, and I'm leaving. It just baffles me how you two missed each other all this time. He'd come in for breakfast and lunch, but you never seemed to meet. Unreal," Lanie said with a frown.

"Delaney, please," Rissa begged. She was as confused as her sister that she'd never met Reece. The gods were playing games with her.

"Nope, Preston just came in too. So, you, my dear sister, are shit out of luck," Lanie said with a grin as she pulled on her coat.

"This is too good. Look, we'll leave so you don't have to face him in front of anyone but please, please tell me later how he reacts when you take his order," Deidra said, pulling on her coat and laughing.

"I absolutely hate you both," Rissa growled as she watched her sisters leave the kitchen and walk to where the men stood talking to Reece as they waited for them. As they all headed out the door, Deidra turned around and waved at her. *Bitches!*

Taking a deep breath, she counted to ten, picked up her pad, walked out of the kitchen, and headed for her cowboy—Reece. He was looking at the menu. He didn't notice her until she stepped in front of him and cleared her throat. She had to before she choked on the lump in it. He glanced up, did a double-take, then his mouth dropped open as he continued to stare at her.

"What would you like?" she asked.

"What are you doing here?"

"I work here. What would you like?" she repeated.

"Did you follow me here?"

She gasped. "Don't flatter yourself. Besides, how would I when I didn't even know your name?"

She watched as he clenched his jaw and a muscle twitched in his cheek. God! The man was so gorgeous.

"You're Rissa. Lanie and Deidra's sister," he muttered.

"Ding. Ding. Ding. Give the man a prize. Do you want to order or not?"

Reece placed his hands on the counter, pushed to his feet, but his eyes narrowed at her. "Not."

She watched him reach for his wallet in his back pocket, and her eyes instinctively went to his crotch. She was sure she was salivating. She knew what was behind that zipper. He pulled out a dollar for the coffee, slapped it on the counter then went out the door and turned to head for the parking lot. She blew out a breath she hadn't realized she'd been holding.

Heading back through the kitchen, she pulled on her coat, hat, and gloves then told her uncle she was going upstairs to check on her cat, Ripley, since there were no customers right now. Pushing the door open, she stepped out and let it close behind her then ran up the metal stairs to her apartment, not even thinking that Nolan could be around. He wasn't going to give up on her going back to New Mexico with him. She was surprised he hadn't been around yet. He must have gone back to Albuquerque, but she knew he'd be back. She'd bet her last dollar on that.

At the top of the stairs, she took a deep breath, inserted her key, opened the door, and stepped inside then locked it. She almost tripped over Ripley because she wasn't concentrating. All she could think about was that her sexy cowboy was right here in Clifton. As if in auto-pilot, she pulled off her cap, gloves, and coat. After hanging them up, she flopped onto her sofa. Ripley jumped up beside her and crawled onto her lap. Rissa stroked her fur, and the cat began to purr.

"What are the odds, Rip? My cowboy is here, right here in Clifton, and I can't even do anything about it. Did I tell you how hot he was?" She grinned when Ripley looked up at her and blinked her eyes. "I think I need just to take a few deep breaths."

She jerked when her cellphone rang and picked it up to see her aunt's number.

"Hi, Aunt Connie. I'll be down in a few minutes."

"No, honey, just stay home. We're closing and leaving. The snow is getting worse, and no one should be out in this. You just relax, and if I can open tomorrow, I'll let you know. With what the weather station is calling for, I doubt it. Are you all right?"

"I'm fine, really. Uh, Ripley wasn't feeling well this morning, so I wanted to check on her." *Liar!*

"All right, hon. I hope she's okay. You know you should have had Owen walk you up. I know it's snowing but Nolan could still be out there waiting for you."

"I know. I'm sorry. It only took me a minute to get here," she said with a grimace. She hated lying.

"I'll call you later. Lock your door. We love you," Connie said.

"I love you both too. Be careful going home." She hit *End* on her phone and tossed it onto the sofa. Swinging her legs up onto the couch, she decided to watch movies for the rest of the afternoon and not think about her cowboy being here.

"Yeah, right," Rissa muttered as she picked up the remote to look for something to watch. "He's right here, in Clifton. He's Reece Maddox and wants nothing to do with me."

Chapter Two

Reece Maddox climbed into his truck and swore so much that he was surprised the air inside his truck didn't turn blue. He wrapped his gloved hands tight around the steering wheel until they hurt.

"What the ever-loving fuck? What are the damn odds that she'd be here? Son of a bitch," he growled out. "Right here, under my nose."

Muttering under his breath, he started the truck then drove out onto the road. Once he got out of town, he noticed the snow coming down heavier, and it looked like the winter storm was planning to stick around. Damn it. He needed all his concentration on getting home without ending up in a ditch. He couldn't believe she was here, and she was Deidra and Lanie's sister. *Darissa.* He'd heard one of the sisters refer to her as Darissa even though they call her Rissa. *Darissa.* A beautiful name for a beautiful woman.

That night had stuck with him for months. Hell, more than months, that night still visited his dreams. Now, with her being here, in Clifton, he wouldn't mind taking up where they'd left off if she was willing. It had been one of the hottest nights of his life. None before or since compared to it. They'd had sex everywhere in that hotel room. He couldn't seem to get enough of her then, and now here she was. He grinned. Maybe it wasn't such a bad thing. He thought about being with her again and it was an enticing idea.

Sure, he'd been a little hot when he saw her appear in front of him at the diner, but that was because having her suddenly appear had surprised him. Shocked him...even horrified him a bit. Now that the shock was wearing off, he was anxious to get back into town to see her again. Would she be open to a sex-only relationship?

When they were together in Helena, he'd made it clear he wasn't the settling down type, so maybe she would. He remembered the day in the diner he swore he saw her but thought it impossible. Now he knew he had. She'd been real. Shaking his head, he wondered how they hadn't met before. He also thought he saw her the other day going into Paige's, the lingerie shop, but he had chastised himself that it was just wishful thinking.

He frowned. There was also a little matter of Nolan McCabe. Would she go back to that little prick? Reece shrugged. It was none of his business, but he didn't want to step on anyone's toes either, even McCabe's. He never fooled with another man's woman but by the sound of it, Rissa didn't want McCabe, but he didn't seem to take the hint. Reece knew there would be a problem if McCabe knew Rissa was seeing him.

Whoa! After that swift departure from the diner, what makes you think she'd want to see you again?

"Not cool, Maddox. Not cool at all," he muttered as he pulled into his driveway. "You might've closed that door already."

He stopped the truck by the side porch. The snow was heavier and starting to accumulate at a rapid pace. It looked like he wouldn't be going back to town for a day or two. Shit. Now he was disappointed. He shouldn't have walked out, but he felt like someone hit him with a hammer when he saw her. Of course, then he accused her of following him when he knew damn well there was no way she could have. They'd never exchanged names, and that was his idea. Yet he'd been so pissed the next morning to find her gone when he got out of the shower. She was the only woman he'd ever wanted to stick around so he could talk to her. He'd decided, right before he fell asleep while holding her, that he'd get her name and number the next morning but while he showered, she took off.

He frowned as he wondered if she'd been involved with McCabe when she had been with him in Helena. He didn't care for cheaters. She had said she wasn't married but she didn't say she wasn't involved with anyone either. That was something he wanted to know if he ever got the chance to ask her.

He climbed the steps then entered the house, and his dog, Skipper, ran to him, and Reece crouched to rub the dog's ears.

"Hey, boy. Do you need to go out?" He laughed when Skipper plopped down. "Smart dog."

Reece straightened up then decided he'd better feed and water the horses for the day. The way the snow was coming down, he wanted to give them extra oats and fill their water buckets. He kept the doors closed to keep it warm inside. Though he only had a few horses, they were his babies, and he always took care of them. Striding to the door, he opened it, stepped onto the porch, and immediately wanted to go back inside. The wind was howling now, and the snow blew sideways. Holding his hat onto his head, he made his way to the barn and stepped inside. His horses stuck their noses over the gates and whinnied at him. He'd been so bored in the house that he decided a trip to town was what he needed, and what happens? He finds *her* at the diner. The horses snorted.

"I know, I'm getting it for you." He made his way to the feed bins, scooped oats into a bucket then fed the horses.

Once they were fed, they ignored him. Shaking his head, he got them fresh water then left the barn. He'd make a fire and relax for the rest of the day. The dark clouds made it seem later than it actually was. As he strode across the yard, the wind blew his coat open. He rarely buttoned it unless he was out in the harsh weather for an extended period, but the snow blowing sideways was making it bitterly cold. He grabbed it closed as he hurried toward the house.

After stomping the snow from his boots, he entered, and sighed at the warmth then removed his hat, coat, and gloves. He stuffed the gloves into a pocket, hung his hat and coat on a peg by the back door then he headed for the living room to make a fire in the hearth.

All he had to do was set a match to the kindling and the orange and blue flames wrapped around the logs, crackling, and snapping as smoke rose up the chimney. Reece took a seat on the sofa, toed off his boots, then swung his legs up onto the couch. Picking up the remote, he aimed it at the TV above the mantle. He had trouble concentrating on the show though. Rissa filled his mind again.

"She was the only woman you thought of trying to find, and now you have. And what do you do? Run like a pussy when you see her." He shook his head. "What were the damn odds? The woman you couldn't forget is here in Clifton."

She was the only woman he was ever interested in getting to know. He frowned. Then again, she hadn't seemed too happy to see him. There had definitely been some attitude there. He stared into the flames and wondered how he could get her to talk to him again and hoped he could convince her to see him.

"She was the one who didn't stick around, so why be pissed at me?" Leaning his head back, he closed his eyes. Well, it was too bad if she was pissed. He wanted to see her again.

He had taken a few days off from his job, where he worked for the Montana Department of Livestock as an agent, since he had a few things to get done on the ranch. He'd been an agent for years and he loved his job, but there were times he needed to work his ranch. Luckily, he had some vacation days saved up. He worked in the theft of livestock division and he was ready to get back to it. He was still on the trail of the rustlers he'd been following in

Helena, but first he needed to get Rissa to talk to him.

Two days later, since the weather had cleared, he drove to town to pick up a new dog collar. The sunshine bounced off the snow, so even pulling the sun visor down didn't help with the glare. He tilted his head back so that the visor, along with his sunglasses helped. The snow was a pain in the ass any way you looked at it. Either it snowed so much you couldn't go anywhere, or it made a mess of the roads once they were plowed, like today, and the snow in the fields and sides of the roads could blind a person when the sun hit it.

"Should just fucking move to Florida," he mumbled then chuckled. He knew that would never happen. He loved his job and his ranch. Yeah, Montana was stuck with him.

He had a flight out to Libby tomorrow since his informant told him where the rustlers were hiding. They needed to be caught. It surprised people how much it still went on nowadays. As he had told Preston, it used to be a hanging offense. That was how many years it had been going on. Maybe the old west had the right idea as far as punishment went for some things.

Frowning, he pulled into the parking lot of the store and looked at all the vehicles parked there. Was it calling for more snow and he hadn't heard? Ranchers and farmers stocked up on feed like some people stocked up on bread and milk. He found a spot and parked. After slamming the truck door shut, he climbed the steps and entered the store. He smiled when he spotted Emma Stone at the counter then headed her way.

"Hey, Emma," he said as he touched the brim of his hat.

"Hi, Reece," she said with a big smile on her beautiful face.

"What are you doing working today?" He leaned an elbow on the counter and smiled.

"Dad needed some help. Junior had to take today off to help his cousin move into a new apartment."

"That ought to be good."

Emma laughed. "Yeah, Junior isn't the sharpest tool in the shed, but he's a sweetheart."

"He's a good kid." Reece straightened. "I need to get some extra feed along with a new dog collar, but I want to look around first. I'll see you in a while."

"I'll be here." She turned to wait on a customer.

He stood staring at the dog collars hanging on the wall and reached for one when he heard his name called. He turned to see Preston.

"What's going on, Preston?"

"Not much. Still busy with the wolves, but it seems the flags did help."

Preston had been having problems with wolves attacking his cattle for a while now. He hated to kill them, so he had figured out another way to keep them away from his cows. He added more rows of wire and hung red plastic flags from it. The only time Preston came close to killing them was four years ago when a pack attacked one of his mares and her colt. The wolves killed the mare, but he was able to save the colt. The horse was four years old now.

"That's good. Is Smoke skittish at all if he sees one?"

Preston grinned. "Nope. He stands there like, come at me. He's a tough one."

"He is. Has anyone else tried to ride him again?" Reece asked, laughing.

"The only one he'll allow on him is Deidra. He loves her." Preston shrugged.

"As you do," Reece said as he reached for a collar.

"I do. She's the best thing to ever happen to me. I know you're a cynic about love, but there are some good women out there. Maybe you just need to look for one."

Reece shook his head, slapped Preston on the shoulder, and started toward the register with the collar. "Ain't happenin'."

"Yeah, I hear a lot of men say that—a lot. I think what happened to them will happen to you. You'll find the right one. I did, and you know I wasn't looking," Preston said.

Blowing out a breath, Reece stopped and looked at his friend.

"You know, I think you have found the right one, but that doesn't mean there's one for me. I'll see you later."

"Hey, Reece. Preston."

Reece turned around to see Erwin 'Pops' Porter standing behind him. Reece stuck his hand out to him.

"Hey, Pops. How are you doing, sir?" Reece asked.

"I'm doing fine, son." Pops grinned.

"Where's Sunny?" Preston asked the older man.

"I'm right here. Don't you be worrying about where I am, Preston Mitchell," Sunny Porter, Pops' wife said as she stepped up beside her husband.

Reece glanced at Preston and they both grinned.

"Yes, ma'am," Preston said.

"You boys getting some things before more snow comes?" Sunny asked them.

"Yes, ma'am," Reece said. "You too?"

"Yeah, Erwin just had to come into town in this damn weather," she said as she narrowed her eyes at Pops.

Reece tried not to grin at the look on Pops' face.

"Damn, woman, why is it always my fault?"

"Because it is." Sunny smiled up at Reece and Preston. "I'm glad you finally decided to get a good woman, Preston." She looked up at Reece. "It's about time you found one and quit banging your way through the state of Montana."

Reece tipped his head down to hide a grin then he glanced at Preston, who was looking everywhere but at him.

"Yes, ma'am," Reece said as he looked at her.

"You boys have a nice day."

"Yes, ma'am. How's Cash?" Preston asked her.

"Fine. Erwin, let's go," she snapped and walked away.

Reece and Preston chuckled as Pops followed her grumbling under his breath.

"She never says more than fine when anyone asks about Cash," Reece said.

"I know. I'd like to know how he is. Hell, *where* he is," Preston muttered.

"I suppose we'll never know because Sunny is too tightlipped about it and God knows if Pops told us, she'd tear him a new one. There's not a man in Clifton, Spring City, or Hartland that she doesn't scare shitless." He looked at Preston and they both laughed.

"I'll see you later, Reece." Preston shook his hand.

Reece nodded and started walking again, then spun around. "Don't forget, Valentine's Day is next week." He laughed when he heard Preston mutter as he headed for another area of the store.

Strolling through the store, he saw Gabe Stone standing at the counter talking with Emma. As he watched, Emma's cheeks turned pink when Gabe whispered something to her. Reece grinned as he walked up to them. Emma smiled shyly at him and nudged Gabe with her elbow. Gabe turned to look at him and grinned.

"Hey, Reece. Guess you caught me flirting with my wife," Gabe said with a grin.

"Nothing wrong with that, Gabe. I'll take this, Emma, and give me two fifty-pound bags of Beckett oats. Please put it on my tab." He placed the collar on the countertop.

Emma smiled and rang up his order. He signed the ticket, picked up the collar, nodded to both Emma and Gabe then turned and strode from the store. As soon as he was outside, he stopped in his tracks. Snow was falling thickly and beginning to accumulate in the parking lot, and as he looked to the street, he could see it starting to get covered too. He should have known that the break in the weather was just a teaser. People who didn't live in this area always thought that spring was on its way if it got nice for one day. He knew better than that. Having lived here all his life, he was used to this.

As he stood on the loading dock staring out at the snow, the door behind him opened, and he glanced back to see Preston step out.

"Holy hell," Preston muttered when he stepped up beside him.

"I didn't think it was calling for snow today."

"Not that I heard. I have to pick up Deidra from the diner, and it looks like it couldn't be at a better time. I'll talk to you soon, Reece."

"Be careful out there, Preston. Tell Deidra hello for me."

"Will do. You be careful too."

He watched as Preston gave him a wave and headed for his truck. The door behind him opened again and he glanced over his shoulder to see Gabe step out.

"It looks like I need to get my ass home," Gabe said.

"Yeah. Where are the kids?" Reece asked.

"With Becca. I dropped them off there since I had to come in here. I'd better go get them before it gets worse. See you later, Reece." Gabe jogged down the steps and headed for his truck.

Reece looked out at the snow covering the street then he walked down the steps, strolled to his pickup, and climbed in. Looked like he'd be staying inside today but he couldn't stop thinking of Rissa. Should he stop by the diner? Hell, he was in town, so why not?

****

Rissa sat on the sofa watching TV with Ripley on her lap. She absentmindedly stroked the cat's thick fur. Hearing the cat purr made her smile. Sighing, she wondered what she was going to do about Nolan. She was terrified of him. Maybe she should take out a restraining order, but knowing him, it wouldn't stop him. If he wanted to get to her, he would. She shivered thinking of how he could really hurt her if she made him mad enough. She should never have gone back to him, but she'd been so lonely and the one man she wanted didn't seem to want her. She envied her sisters so much. They both had wonderful men who loved them deeply. *God!* Why couldn't she have that?

Leaning her head back, she closed her eyes. She was so tired. She'd barely slept since knowing Nolan could be in town, and then to find out her cowboy was here too was going to bring her many more sleepless nights. She still couldn't get over Reece Maddox being her hot cowboy. She thought back to that night again. They'd had sex everywhere in his suite. In the shower, on the floor, in the bed, and against the wall. The next morning, when the alarm on his phone went off, he sat up, ran his hand down her back and over her ass, then climbed out of bed and headed for the bathroom. When she heard the shower running, she was so tempted to join him, but when she looked at her phone to check the time, she knew she had to get moving. She had to return the horse to the ranch. She'd worked for a ranch as a barrel racer, and she rode their horses in competitions. Jenna expected the animal back by noon, and Rissa had a three-hour drive to accomplish that.

She'd rolled out of bed and searched for her clothes and found everything, except her panties. She didn't have time to look for them. She dressed, put her shoes on, then pulled a sheet of paper out of her purse, wrote her name and number on it, and placed it on the dresser. She looked for his cellphone but didn't see it, so she searched the nightstand on the other side of the bed and the small table. It was nowhere to be found. *Where could it be?* It had been the alarm on his phone that buzzed. He must have taken it into the bathroom with him. She was just going to add her number to it if she could. Did he think she was going to steal it? At first, the idea of it angered her but then she realized he didn't really know her. He might know every inch of her *body,* but he didn't know *her.* As she walked to the door, she glanced over her shoulder and hoped like hell he called.

He never called though, and her heart had been shattered. How could two people so in tune with each other and have that much heat between them not see each other again? She should have opened the bathroom door and told him she had to go because she had been running so late. She could've explained that she knew if she didn't get to the arena and load the horse right away, she wouldn't get the horse back to Jenna in time, and she knew Jenna would think she couldn't depend on her again. But she'd simply left.

Sitting up, she rubbed her eyes, yawned, and stretched. Damn him. Why hadn't he called? She'd been so upset and vulnerable that she let

Nolan talk her into going back to him. What a mistake that had been. She got to her feet and headed for the coat rack. She decided to head downstairs and work a little while. She was too bored, and Reece kept invading her thoughts. Maybe if she worked, he'd leave her alone for a while. *Yeah, right.*

After pulling on her coat, beanie, and gloves, she opened the door, closed it behind her, locked it then walked down the steps and around to the front. Entering the diner, she glanced around then made her way to the kitchen, removed her gloves, hat, and coat then hung them up. She turned to look at her uncle while he stood at the grill, cleaning it.

"It's so empty out there," Rissa said as she hopped up on a stool.

"With the winter storm warning, not many are out."

"Another warning?" she asked in disbelief.

"Yes, for the next two days. It's not bad out now, but another one is predicted."

"Did you come down here by yourself?" Connie asked her as she entered the kitchen. "You're not even scheduled for today."

"I was bored. If Nolan is around, I hope he stays away. I hope he heard about the severe weather and stays inside. I don't know why anyone would be out if a warning's been issued."

"I imagine a few will come into town to get some things they'll need. You know how that goes. Winter storm warning means you need more milk and bread." Owen chuckled.

"I think we should close soon. I doubt if anyone is going to be coming in. Two days of this weather and the towns will be at a standstill. Maybe another hour, then we'll close." Connie looked at Owen.

"Whatever you say, baby, you're the boss," he said and winked at Rissa.

"I'll go clean the coffee pots and if someone comes in, I can just make a small pot, but I doubt if anyone does." Rissa smiled.

"True, but I'd hate to close then someone wants something to eat. We'll give it an hour or two."

"Now it's an hour or *two*. Pretty soon, she'll have us here all day," Owen teased.

She hugged her aunt. "However long you want me here. I don't have anything else to do."

As she was picking up a coffee carafe, she was surprised when she heard the bell jingle, and looked out to see Trent taking a seat on a stool then headed for him.

"Hi, Trent," she said. "Are you alone?"

"Yes, ma'am. I thought I'd get a burger to go while I had the chance. I had to pick up some supplies. Snow just started so I don't want to stay too long."

"Your usual?" When he nodded, she wrote it down, pinned it to the wheel, and spun it around.

A few minutes later, she was laughing at Trent as he told her about Lanie getting her feet stuck in the mud on his property.

"She lost her shoe, and I had to dig it out for her," Trent said, shaking his head.

"Did my little sister turn the air blue?"

"Oh yeah, and not in a quiet voice either. I'm surprised y'all didn't hear her in here." Trent chuckled.

She was about to answer when the bell above the door rang, and she glanced over to see Reece enter. He gave her a brief nod then took a seat beside Trent. Taking a deep breath, she looked at him.

"Would you like to order?" *Damn it. I can be nice.*

"Coffee and a burger with everything...please," he said as he stared at her.

Nodding, she could feel the heat pour into her cheeks as she turned away to pin his order to the wheel. She picked up the coffee carafe and made her way back to him to hear Trent telling him about Lanie losing her shoe. When Reece chuckled, she swore she could hear it in her ear just like when they'd been alone together in his room. *No! Don't go there.*

Clearing her throat, she poured him a cup of coffee then quickly made her way to the kitchen. She had to get away from him, or she'd crawl across the counter and straddle the man. She climbed up on the stool and watched as her uncle prepared the burgers. She just hoped she could walk out there without dropping it. Oh, this was going to drive her insane. How could she see him and not let him know she still wanted him? He didn't seem to have a problem being around her all of a sudden. Hell. When he'd chuckled earlier, it took her back to his hotel room when she told him he was one hung cowboy and he'd laughed against her ear. Shuddering, she knew she had to stop thinking about that night, it was all she'd done for months. It was also what made her realize that she didn't love Nolan and likely never had.

The times Nolan had belittled her hadn't helped either. No man should talk to anyone like that. Especially to a woman and she'd been such a fool to go back to him. She knew how women were afraid to leave because the man thought he owned her, and he could do whatever he wanted. She was his property. *Not this girl. No way. No how. Never again.* Nolan needed to stay away from her, or she'd talk to Sam about a restraining order. She wasn't even sure that would stop Nolan from trying to convince her to go back with him. He didn't love her he just didn't want anyone else to have her. What would he do if he found out about Reece? She was sure he'd confront him, and it wouldn't go well. Reece was a big man, but that wouldn't stop Nolan. She'd been surprised he'd actually walked away when Preston told him to leave one day in the diner.

She really hoped Nolan would get the message but in the back of her mind, she knew he wouldn't. The signs had always been there, but she thought she was in love and ignored them. Her parents had been shocked that she allowed him to talk to her the way he had. Verbal abuse could be as bad as physical abuse, and sometimes more damaging. She had been raised to know better. Her mother had told her daughters never to let a man raise his hand to them or talk down to them, but Rissa had allowed it. She had dreaded the day she had to tell her parents but they had deserved to know the truth about Nolan. At first, all they knew was she'd broken it off with him and didn't want him back. They understood, but when she told them the truth her father had been livid and her mother not much calmer. She had been happy with Nolan, at first, but the more he started spending time with his friends, and ignoring her, she knew something was wrong in the relationship. She was the *little woman* and he expected her to be at his beck and call.

When she finally stood up to him, he had shoved her. That had been the biggest fight they had ever had. They'd had arguments but nothing like that. Then he got angry when she told him she was coming to Clifton to spend Christmas with her family. He *demanded* she stayed at home while he traveled to Vail for skiing. It made her wonder if he had been seeing another woman and now, she'll never know because it would be a cold day in hell before she would ask. She just didn't care anymore. She heard the bell above the door ring and was happy to see a few more people come in. The more here, the less she had to deal with Reece.

Huffing out a breath, she watched as her uncle put Reece's burger on a bun with all the fixings. He set it on a plate then turned to her and grinned.

"Ready, kiddo," he said.

Hopping down from the stool, she picked up the plate, took a deep breath, blew it out, and walked out of the kitchen to head for Reece. She hesitated when she saw him sitting there alone. Where was Trent? She quickly glanced around and knew he had left when she saw money lying on his ticket. She had been so lost in her thoughts that she missed her aunt taking him his to-go order. *Damn it!* She was hoping he'd be a buffer.

Moving closer to where Reece sat, she picked up the carafe again to refill his cup then headed to him. She set his plate down in front of him, filled his cup, then picked up Trent's money. She grinned as she noticed the tip. The man was going to be her brother-in-law, but he always left a tip for her and her sisters. Even Lanie.

"Rissa?"

"Yes?" she said as she opened the cash register drawer.

"Are you ever going to talk to me?"

She slammed the drawer closed and turned to face Reece.

"Excuse me? I'm not the one who took off like a bat out of hell when you saw me here."

"No, but you were the one who did the morning after we..." He waved his hand.

"I had to get going. I had a long drive in front of me. I had to get the horse I'd ridden in competition back to its owner by noon...and you could have called," she growled out.

"How the hell could I call? I didn't have your number and didn't know your name," he snapped.

"I left you my number." She folded her arms and narrowed her eyes.

"Bullshit," he muttered.

She gasped. "I did!"

"Where?" His raised eyebrow told her he didn't believe her.

"It doesn't matter."

"Because you didn't leave it."

Placing her hands on the counter, she leaned closer to him.

"I wrote it on a piece of paper and put it on the dresser," she said through clenched teeth.

"The dresser? Really? Well, I didn't see it when I came back into the room." He looked down at his burger.

She straightened up. "Well, it was there. Why would I say it was if it wasn't?"

"I was pissed when I came out and found you were gone so I just packed and got the hell out of there. It's possible I missed it. Hell, I even looked for you in the lobby." He looked up at her and scowled. "All the same, you apparently couldn't get out of there fast enough."

"Just why were you so pissed? You're the one who said it was for one night," she growled out.

"And you fucking agreed. I was hoping to talk to you after I got out of the shower."

"I just told you I had to go. Besides, you made it clear it was a one-night stand." She shrugged.

"Yeah, I know what the fuck I said, but I also changed my mind and right before I fell asleep, I thought about getting your name. In. The. Morning. But you were gone."

She threw her hands in the air. "How in the hell would I know that?"

"You could have come into the bathroom and told me you were leaving and given me your number then."

"Again. You said it was a one-night stand."

"Is there a problem out here?" Owen asked as he stepped from the kitchen.

"No, Uncle Owen."

"No, sir," Reece answered.

Owen stared at them then went back into the kitchen. She sighed. This was getting them nowhere. But to know he'd thought about getting her name made her want to do a happy dance. She looked at him again.

"How about we start over?" He reached his hand out. "Hi, I'm Reece Maddox."

"I have to get back to work." She started to move away when his voice stopped her again.

"Rissa, I'd like to see you again," he said.

"Another one-night stand? I don't think so."

"More than one night."

She placed her arms on the counter then stared into his face. That gorgeous face.

"Just sex, right?"

"Of course. I told you I wasn't the settling down type."

"Well, Reece Maddox, I'll have to give it some thought because I *am* the settling down type."

Rissa turned from him, mostly to hide a satisfied grin then headed for the kitchen and didn't look back until she heard the bell above the door ring. She glanced back to see him leave. His uneaten lunch sat on the counter with money beside it. With a deep sigh, she turned around, headed to where he had sat, and picked up the money.

Chapter Three

The next day, she poured coffee for the patrons who had come in for breakfast. It was busy, and she and Lanie were buzzing around the place taking care of customers. The snow hadn't amounted to what was predicted, but more was on the way. The bell over the door jingled and she glanced that way to see Katie and Riley Madison enter. Riley was carrying their little girl, Sadie, and Katie, with her baby bump leading the way, waved at her as they weaved through the tables to head for a booth.

"I'll take them. You get Reece," Lanie said as she nudged her.

Rissa whipped her head toward the door and saw him taking a seat at the counter. He must have come in behind Katie and Riley and she hadn't seen him.

"You take Reece," she whispered to Lanie.

"Nope." Lanie winked and walked away.

"Damn it," she mumbled.

Taking a deep breath, she walked behind the counter then made her way to where he sat. Picking up a coffee cup, she set it in front of him and poured him a mug full.

"Do you know what you want?" she asked.

Reece looked up at her and a slow grin lifted his lips.

Damn those sexy lips.

"Of course, I know what I want. Do you?"

That smug sexy look on his face made her just want to crawl over the counter and ride him. Closing her eyes, she remembered doing just that on the floor of the hotel room.

When he chuckled, her eyes flew open. *Two can play this game.*

"Oh, yeah, cowboy. I definitely know what I want. Too bad you don't want the same thing," she whispered low to keep from being overheard, and almost laughed when the smile left his face and his eyes narrowed. Leaning in closer, she stared into his eyes. "If you change your mind, you know where to find me."

She turned away from him, walked toward the kitchen with a little more sway in her hips, then stopped to glance back at him. She winked, entered the kitchen, and jumped up on the stool with a big smile on her face.

"I thought you didn't want to wait on him?" Lanie asked with a grin.

Rissa laughed. "I didn't but I think I just gave him a dose of his own medicine."

Lanie leaned close to her. "He really is hot."

"Oh, you have no idea." She hopped off the stool and looked out through the pass-through window into the diner.

"Are you going for it?"

"I'm not sure. I can see a heartbreak coming if I get involved with him." She shook her head. "One night with him wasn't enough but he has no desire to settle down. Plus, the fact I just got out of a relationship. It's probably too soon."

"What you had with Nolan wasn't a relationship, it was a jail sentence. He thought he ruled you," Lanie said.

"I know, but Reece doesn't want anything more than just sex."

"Hey, you never know, maybe you can change his mind. When you have that much chemistry with a man, it can't stay as a onetime thing. Trust me, I know."

"You two need to quit whispering and get back to work," Deidra said as she entered the kitchen.

Lanie laughed. "We'll tell you about it later."

"So, I see Reece is here..."

"Yes. I guess I need to take his order." Rissa grinned, pulled her pad from her pocket, and strolled to where Reece sat, with Preston now sitting beside him.

"Good morning, Preston." She poured him a cup of coffee.

"Good morning, Rissa. How are you?"

She glanced at Reece then back to Preston.

"I'm feeling terrific. You?"

Preston looked at Reece then back to her and a frown marred his brow.

"Uh, yeah, I'm good. By the way, have you two met? Reece, this is Deidra's sister, Rissa—"

"Um...yeah, we've met...so did you need to order?"

"No, ma'am. Deidra is getting it." Preston kept watching them as if waiting for something to happen.

She smiled then folded her arms on the counter and leaned close to Reece.

"And how about you, Reece? Do you need...something?" She watched him fight back a grin.

"I do, but it's not on the menu. For now, I'll take an order of scrambled eggs, bacon, and toast."

"Got it. I'll get right on that and it's too bad what you really want isn't on the menu." Rissa straightened up, smiled then wrote down the order, put it on the wheel, and spun it around. After looking at him one more time, she sashayed to the kitchen.

****

"You want to tell me what the fuck all of that was about?" Preston asked him.

Reece picked up his coffee cup. "Nope."

"Do you two know each other? Did I miss something?"

Reece set his cup down, turned on the stool, placed his elbow on the counter, and looked at Preston. "Remember the hot woman I told you I met in Helena?"

"Yes." Preston frowned then Reece watched as it dawned on him. "Rissa?"

"Yep." Reece turned his stool to face the counter.

"Son of a bitch. But you said you didn't know Rissa before."

"I didn't know she was the same woman since I hadn't met her yet. I came in here a few days ago and she was here. I was pissed at first but now, not so much. It's just so hard to believe we kept missing each other when I'd come in here."

"Unbelievable." Preston picked up his cup and sipped the hot coffee. He set the cup down and looked at Reece. "You hurt her, friend, and I'll kick your ass. I know how you are, Reece.

You don't settle down. You just look for a new bed to put your boots under."

"It doesn't matter. She's not interested in just sex."

"Hell, that leaves you out." The bell rang above the door, so Preston glanced in that direction. "Son of a bitch," Preston growled, making Reece look over his shoulder to see Nolan McCabe enter.

"That little dick needs someone to get it through his head that she doesn't want him here." Reece clenched his jaw.

"We've all tried. Maybe if he finds out she's been with you, he'll back off."

Reece stared at Nolan as he took a seat at the counter and looked at him with a smirk. Reece made to stand but Preston stopped him.

"Not here."

"Right." Reece resumed his seat.

The bell jangled again, and Reece glanced over to see Noah Conway, Dominic Blackstone, and Boone Evans enter. The men took seats on the other side of Preston.

"Hey, Noah, Boone. Dom. How goes it?" Preston asked.

"Good. How are you doing, Preston? Reece?" Noah said, and Boone and Dom nodded at them.

"Good, thanks," Reece said.

"I'm good." Preston lifted his cup to take a sip of coffee.

"Busy in here this morning," Noah said as he looked around.

Reece and Preston had known Noah, Dom, and Boone practically all their lives. They were all good friends who attended school together since elementary school. Noah was much the same as Reece. He wasn't interested in settling down since he'd been through three engagements. Noah didn't seem to have much luck in the love department even though he tried. Boone was single and mostly stayed on his ranch. Dom was a quiet man. He'd been through a lot and he kept to himself. He worked as a manager at a ranch owned by Jeb and Laura Carson. Like Reece, he never seemed to stay with one woman too long.

"You seeing anyone?" Reece asked Noah and watched a slow grin lift his lips, making him, Dom, and Preston chuckle.

"I'll take that as a yes," Preston said.

"Yeah, I'm seeing someone but not looking to settle down," Noah said.

Reece laughed. "Same answer mine would be if I was asked that question about a woman."

"I think you're far worse than me, Reece." Noah chuckled.

"That saddle you made for me is great," Preston said.

"I'm glad you're happy with it. That one took a while." Noah shook his head and blew out a breath as if still tired from the work.

"Why? Did he want it all fancy?" Reece teased.

"A little. It did turn out nice though. He was just lucky I had one started and the customer canceled, or he wouldn't have gotten one that soon. I was just about finished it when the customer said he couldn't afford it after all. All I had to do was add some blue stitching."

"Deidra loved it," Preston said.

"Hi, Noah. Dom. Boone." Deidra stood in front of them, ignoring McCabe then poured them each a cup of coffee.

"Deidra, when are you going to leave this big lug and run off with me?" Noah picked up his cup and laughed when Preston choked on his coffee.

"Back the fuck off, Conway."

"He's harmless, Noah." Deidra winked at Preston.

"Maybe to you he is, but I've seen him in action."

"Oh, I've seen him in action too," Deidra said with a laugh and set Preston's breakfast down in front of him, leaned over the counter, and kissed him.

Reece laughed when Preston gave a satisfied grin as did Boone, Dom, and Noah.

****

Rissa wrung her hands together waiting for her uncle to get Reece's order ready. She just didn't know what to do about him. She'd love to be with him again but was he worth risking a broken heart? Maybe he was worth it. The sex had been so good, incredible. Could she pass that up? It was when she looked through the pass-through window that she saw Nolan at the counter and gasped.

"What's wrong?" Owen asked her.

"Nolan is here."

"Damn it," Owen muttered and set his spatula down. "I want him out of here."

"No, please, leave him alone, Uncle Owen. Eventually, he'll get the point."

"I doubt it."

"Don't go out there. Nolan is here," Deidra said when she entered the kitchen.

"I know. I've got to take Reece's breakfast to him."

"I can do it," Deidra said.

"No, I can. I have to let Nolan know I'm not interested in going back to him, and I plan to walk past him like he doesn't exist." Rissa picked up the tray and after taking a deep breath, she carried it out to the counter and strode past Nolan without looking at him.

"Darissa, we need to talk," Nolan said as she passed by.

"Fuck off," she muttered just loud enough for him to hear then grinned when he hissed in a breath.

Getting to where Reece sat, she set the tray down on the counter behind her, picked up his plate then set it in front of him.

"Are you all right, Rissa?" Preston asked her.

She glanced at Nolan, back to Preston, and nodded.

"I will not let him intimidate me. Not anymore."

"Just say the word and I'll kick his ass. We go back a ways," Reece muttered.

"I wish you could, but he has a black belt in karate."

"So what?"

"Yeah, as I said, I don't care what color his belt is, I'd love to bust him once," Preston said.

"Darissa," Nolan called out to her, but she ignored him.

"You need to find somewhere else to eat," Reece said loud enough for the man to hear him.

"I can go where I want. If you have a problem with that, let's take this outside," Nolan said with a sneer.

Reece got to his feet. "Anytime, you little prick. Anytime."

The bell jangled making Rissa look over to see Sam enter and she let out a sigh of relief. Sam's eyes narrowed at Nolan then he took a seat at the counter. She watched him look up at Reece.

"Problem, Reece?" Sam asked him.

Reece resumed his seat. "No, Sam. No problem."

"Keep it that way. I can't run him out of town unless he does something, but you starting shit with him will only get *you* in trouble, not him."

Reece blew out a breath. "I get it."

"Eat your breakfast, Reece. Thank you, but please don't antagonize him," she said in a low tone of voice.

"I am not afraid of him. I just need one punch. Just one."

She placed her hand over his, and he looked up at her.

"Please."

"All right, but if he ever starts something, I *will* finish it."

Rissa took a deep breath and looked at Sam.

"Coffee, Sheriff?"

"Yes, please. I need something to warm me up. Damn cold out."

"I would think you'd rather have Tess do that," Noah teased.

Sam chuckled. "No doubt there, but she's in surgery this morning. She actually left the house before I did, or I would have had her...warm me up."

Reece, Preston, and Boone laughed, and she simply shook her head. She noticed that Sam and Dom didn't speak or even look at each other. What was that about?

"Enjoy your breakfast," she said to Reece then headed back to the kitchen.

She was about to get herself a cup of coffee when Nolan appeared in the doorway.

"We're going to talk, Darissa. Eventually," he said.

"How many times do I have to tell you to leave me alone? I am not going back to Albuquerque. I'm happy here."

"And how many times do *I* have to tell you to stay the hell out of my kitchen?" Owen stepped up beside her.

"Back off, old man," Nolan snapped.

"Listen—"

"Get the hell out of here," Reece exclaimed cutting off Owen's words.

She watched as Nolan took a deep breath then turned to face Reece. He had to look up because Reece had about six inches on him. *Six inches and a hell of a lot more.* She snorted and everyone turned to look at her. She shrugged. Reece frowned at her then looked at Nolan again.

"I said get out. Rissa is not going back with you and you need to man up about it. And don't ever speak to Owen like that again or you and I are going to have more problems. Show some fucking respect."

"Oh, you and I already have plenty of problems, cowboy."

Reece moved his coat back to show his holstered gun.

Nolan looked at the gun, then to her. "This is not over."

Reece stepped aside to let him out and once he passed, he turned to face her.

"Rissa? Are you all right?"

"Yes. I'm just getting tired of this. He needs to go away. I'm tired of even thinking about him."

Reece stepped closer to her and put his lips close to her ear. "I can take your mind off him."

She looked up at him and smiled when he raised an eyebrow. What a sucker she was for a man who raised that one eyebrow.

"For how long, Reece?"

"I have no idea. I won't make promises I can't keep." He sighed. "Look, I have to look through some cases but let me call you later. Give me your number, please."

"Cases? What's with the gun? Are you a policeman or something?"

"Or something. We'll talk later. Number...please."

She told him her number and watched as he entered it into his phone. He touched the brim of his hat, nodded, and walked out. She saw him slap Preston and the other men on their backs, shook Sam's hand, then left the diner.

"Preston wants to kick Nolan's ass," Deidra said from beside her.

"He'll have to get in line. Hey, who are the other men beside Noah?"

"Boone Evans and Dominic Blackstone. Boone is the one next to Noah."

"They're both hot."

Deidra laughed. "Very. Big men. They're both as tall as Preston and all muscle too."

"I bet they're big men, and Dominic has that brooding cowboy thing going on," Rissa whispered, laughing.

"Okay, quit your whispering and giggling, and get back to work. Don't make me crack the whip," Owen said.

"Oh, please. What whip?" Deidra winked at her then left the kitchen to take orders.

Rissa got back to work too. More people came in throughout the day and it stayed busy, which was good for her because it kept her mind off the thought of Reece calling her. She knew she was heading for heartache, but she wasn't sure if she could resist him now, any more than when she slept with him in Helena. She mentally snorted. Of course, they had hardly slept at all. She frowned, wondering why he carried a gun. Of course, it was legal in Montana, so maybe he just liked having one.

Hours later, she sat in the kitchen with her shoes off, rubbing her feet. She loved working at the diner though. She'd met so many wonderful people from Clifton, Spring City, and Hartland. It still amazed her that Reece lived here. Her cowboy lived *here*, in Clifton. Was it meant to be? She'd had only one serious boyfriend before Nolan, and that jackass had cheated on her. She was pretty certain that Nolan hadn't cheated but after the way he treated her, she wished he had so he'd go back to the other woman and leave her alone. Taking a deep breath, Rissa put her sneakers back on, got down from the stool, washed her hands in the dish sink, and picked up the orders. The lunch crowd was as busy as breakfast had been.

****

Reece sat at the desk in his home office looking at the computer screen, checking his emails then reviewed any cases that were still open. A few new cases recently opened, and he was more than ready to get back to work in the field. It had been two months since he'd heard anything about the rustlers he'd been trailing. Last he had heard, they were in Libby, Montana but it was as if they'd dropped off the radar. He needed to find another case for now and worry about finding them later. He just wanted to catch them before they did something stupid, other than stealing those bulls.

A case caught his eye on a few stolen horses in Hartland. Why hadn't his boss called him about this one? Reaching for the phone, he called the office.

"Montana Department of Livestock, how may I direct your call?" a feminine voice answered.

"Hello, Ruby, it's Reece."

"Hi, Reece. How are you doing?"

"I'm good. Ready to get back in the field. This snow is giving me cabin fever. Is Dave in?"

"Let me see if he's in his office," Ruby replied.

Reece chuckled. "You're talking to one of his agents. I know you can see his office from your desk."

"Smartass," she whispered with a laugh. "Hold on."

"Reece? How are you doing?" Dave Markell asked when he came on the line.

"I'm going crazy, boss. Since those rustlers have disappeared on me, I need to do something so send me to Hartland."

"You're looking at open cases, aren't you?"

"Guilty. Maybe you never should have told me I could work from home once in a while. Now, come on. I'm just across the county line from Hartland. I need to get out there."

"You still have the other case, Reece—"

"I can't get to Libby with the weather the way it is and I'm not even sure that's where they are. My CI has been trying to find them but no luck, so give me this. Seriously."

"All right, but if it gets to where you can travel, you drop this one and go."

"Yes, sir."

As Reece hung up, he could hear his boss laughing. Sighing, he shut the computer down, pushed the chair back, stood then walked from the room. He headed down the hallway to the kitchen to see about getting something to eat.

Yanking on the fridge door, he peered in but saw nothing that appealed to him. Shoving it closed, he decided to give Rissa a call and see if she wanted to go to dinner. He looked at the clock to see it was almost four. If he wanted to take her to dinner in Hartland, he'd have to make a reservation soon. Knowing the owner of the restaurant, he was able to get in at the last minute. Several of his friends could too, but he needed to get in touch with Rissa first.

After finding his cellphone, he hit *Send* on her number and waited while it rang. He was about to hang up or wait for voicemail when she answered, sounding out of breath.

"Hello," Rissa said.

"Hey, did I catch you at a bad time?"

"Reece? Oh, hi. We're busy."

"I won't keep you then. I just wanted to know if you'd like to go out to dinner this evening."

"I'm not sure it's a good idea."

"I think it's a hell of an idea. It's just dinner, Rissa." Damn, she was stubborn. He grinned when her sigh came across the line.

"All right. Where?"

"I know this great little diner that serves the best burgers you'll ever eat." He did his best not to laugh.

"Yeah, find another date," Rissa snapped.

He chuckled. "I'm kidding. We could go into Hartland. I'll have to make a reservation for six o'clock. I'll pick you up at five-thirty, is that all right?"

"Sounds good. Is it a fancy place? I just want to know what to wear."

"You can wear whatever you want. Dress, jeans, or slacks. I've seen women in just about anything in there."

"Are you sure you can get a reservation this late?"

"I know the owner. All I have to do is call him if I can't get in."

"Okay. I'll see you later then."

After he disconnected his call with Rissa, he called the restaurant but they told him there were no openings. He hung up, scrolled through his phone then hit *Send*.

"Hey, Reece," Grant Hunter said when he answered.

"I need to get into the restaurant tonight," Reece said.

"So, you're only calling me so I can get you in, is that it?"

"Damn right. Why else would I call you, Hunter?" Reece grinned when he heard his friend chuckle.

"All right, I'll call you right back. What time?"

"Six, please."

"You got it." Grant hung up. But only a few minutes passed before his cellphone buzzed, and he answered. "You're in. You owe me, Maddox."

"Add it to the list." Reece grinned.

"Hell, that list is mighty long now." Grant chuckled. "Enjoy your evening."

"Thanks, Grant. I appreciate it."

"No problem."

Reece disconnected, then he decided to head to the barn and work a little. He couldn't do much with this damn snow, but he could feed and water the horses. He just hoped the snow didn't amount to much more. He wanted to see Rissa tonight.

"Come on, Skipper. Let's get out of this house."

****

Rissa glanced at the clock to see it was close to four-thirty. She had an hour before Reece picked her up.

"Aunt Connie? Is it okay if I go now?"

"Sure, honey. Meredith is due any minute now. Enjoy your weekend."

She hugged her aunt, pulled her apron off, walked into the kitchen then tugged on her coat, hat, and gloves.

"Let me finish this burger and I'll walk you up," Owen stated.

"I'll be fine. Really." She waved at her uncle then walked out the back door to see it snowing. She started up the metal stairs and prayed it didn't keep Reece from taking her to dinner. She came to a stop when Nolan said her name and appeared from around the corner. She turned around and looked at him.

"Go away, Nolan," she said in a shaky voice. Why had she told her uncle she'd be fine?

"We're going to talk, Darissa. One way or another," he said as he stepped forward.

She took a step up and watched a smirk lift his lips. What had she ever seen in him?

"I've said all I needed. We're done."

"We're done when I say we are." He moved closer and she backed up another step.

"She said she didn't want to talk so I suggest you move along, McCabe."

Rissa sighed with relief when she saw Deputy Brody Morgan leaning against the building. Snow covered the brim of his hat and the shoulders of his coat. He looked relaxed, but she noticed he had his hand on his holstered weapon. When Nolan turned to look at him, Brody unsnapped the retention strap holding his weapon in the holster.

"I can't see where any of this concerns you, Deputy."

"That's Deputy *Morgan* to you, and it concerns me if the lady says she has nothing to say but you won't move your sorry ass along."

Nolan turned to look at her. "This isn't over."

She blew out a breath when he headed down the alleyway.

"I thought you were supposed to have someone walk you upstairs?" Brody tilted his head as he looked at her.

"Uncle Owen was busy, and I have a date, so I wanted to get home to get ready."

Brody grinned and she was still in awe of how many good-looking men were in the area. Brody stood about six-four, with black hair, and brown eyes that peered out from behind glasses which did nothing to take away from his looks. He was also married and head over heels in love with his wife and little boy.

"I get that, but don't do it again. I just happened to be driving by when I saw him walking down the alley, heading this way."

"Thank you. I was wondering how fast I could get up the stairs without him catching me."

"Then that should tell you not to do this again. Right?" He raised an eyebrow at her.

"Yes, sir."

"Go on up. I'll wait until you're inside. And make sure you lock the door."

"All right. Thank you again." She turned and ran up the stairs. At the top, she waved, inserted her key, entered her apartment, then locked the door behind her. Ripley stared up at her.

Thank God Brody happened by. She knew he was right. She wasn't supposed to leave alone with Nolan still hanging around Clifton, but she'd been so anxious to get to her apartment and make herself presentable for Reece. She just wished she knew what had made Nolan change so much. Their relationship had been good in the beginning, but later he wanted to spend more time with friends but didn't want to let her go. She was not his property, but he made her feel that she couldn't do anything without his permission. Shaking her head, she wondered why some people acted that way. She was a grown woman and could do what she wanted. She'd never go back to him. There was no way she'd ever live like that again. No man had a right to think he owned a woman any more than a woman thought she owned a man. She had a feeling Reece would never be like that. But then again, Reece Maddox didn't *want* to own a woman. He just wanted one for sex.

She headed for the bathroom to take a shower and then she'd get ready for her date with Reece. *A date with Reece.* The thought made her smile.

She opened her closet then stared at the clothes hanging there. As she moved them along the rod, she wondered what would happen after dinner. She pushed the door closed. She'd decide what to wear after her shower.

"Nothing. Nothing will happen. You're an idiot for even going to dinner with the man. You're going to end up with a broken heart because you're not getting anything from Reece Maddox but sex," she said aloud then shrugged. "Really great sex."

After she entered the bathroom, she turned on the water in the shower, undressed, and stepped inside the stall. Ripley jumped up onto the counter and proceeded to lick her paws. Rissa washed her hair good then scrubbed her body thoroughly with strawberry bodywash since she smelled like the diner.

After her shower, she wrapped the towel around her, used the blow dryer on her hair then put it up in a bun with wisps of hair framing her face. She entered her bedroom and opened the closet door again. Smiling, she pulled out the green sweater dress Deidra had bought when she was first seeing Preston. All three sisters, as well as their cousin, Sloane, could wear each other's shoes and clothes.

Rissa put on a mint green bra and matching panties then pulled the dress on, tugged up the zipper, and reached into the closet for the black suede knee-high boots. These also belonged to Deidra, but she'd left them here for her in case she wanted to wear them. She took a seat on the bed, pulled the boots on, zipped them then got to her feet.

As she checked her image in the mirror, she decided that there was no way Reece was getting her into bed tonight. She nodded at her reflection. She might be an idiot to go out to dinner with him, but she drew the line at hopping into his bed. *Already did that.* But to say the man knew what he was doing in bed would be an understatement. Every time they'd had sex, he made sure she was good and satisfied before he took his own pleasure. But not tonight. There would be no jumping into bed with Reece Maddox. *Nope. Nope. Nope.*

"Yeah, who are you trying to convince?" she asked herself.

At five-thirty, a knock sounded on her door. She got to her feet, took a deep breath, smoothed the dress down, and walked to the door. She peeked through the peephole to see Reece standing on the landing, staring at the door. It seemed as if he was looking right at her. She opened the door and stared at the sexiest man she'd ever seen. His shearling coat hung open and she could see his blue dress shirt tucked into dark blue jeans. On his feet were distressed cowboy boots and a black cowboy hat covered his head. The brim of his hat and the shoulders of his coat were covered with snow.

"Hi," she said.

"Hi yourself," he said in a low tone of voice. His eyes ran down her dress to her feet and back to her eyes. "You look gorgeous."

"Thank you. Come in while I get my coat." She opened the door wider and he stepped inside.

"Yes, ma'am."

She smiled as she took her coat down from the coat rack. She was about to put it on when Reece took it from her and held it for her.

"Thank you."

"You're welcome, darlin'. Let's go get some food in us."

"By the way...I'm Darissa Gates, but everyone calls me, Rissa," she said as she stared up into the most beautiful blue eyes she'd ever seen. "And I am hungry."

"Nice to meet you, Rissa. I'm starving," he murmured, and she knew he didn't mean for food.

"Behave yourself."

"Where's the fun in that?"

"True," she said with a laugh.

"Holy hell, that's a big cat."

She turned to look at Ripley as she made her way to the sofa and jumped up on it then stared at the humans like they were beneath her as she lifted a paw and licked it.

"That's Ripley."

"Yeah, I've heard about her from Deidra, but I didn't realize the cat was big enough to take down a bear."

She laughed. "She's harmless except around Nolan. She hisses at him. He says he's the one who rescued her. I did. He just told his friends that, so he could look like a good person."

"It would take a hell of a lot more than adopting an animal to make him look good."

"Deidra and Lanie don't like him either. By the way, I told them I was going to dinner with you."

"Did they try to talk you out of it? I'm sure Preston has told Deidra all about me."

"He did, but it's my decision. I'm twenty-eight years old. I can do what I want."

"Preston is one of my closest friends, but he knows how I feel about relationships and love." He frowned. "Are you sure you're okay with that?"

"I'm not sure at all, Reece. Let's just have dinner. Okay?"

"All right. Let's go." He opened the door.

Rissa made sure it was locked and stepped out onto the stoop. He pulled the door closed behind them then waited as she locked the deadbolt, took her hand and led her down the stairs to his truck. They drove to the restaurant in silence, but she was all right with that.

Once inside the restaurant, the hostess led them to a table, took their drink orders, then left to get them. Reece helped her remove her coat, hung it on the back of her chair then removed his own and then his hat. After hanging his coat on the back of his chair, he set his hat on the empty chair beside his. She looked at the menu but couldn't decide on what to get. It seemed a little pricey to her.

"It's expensive here," she muttered.

"Get what you want. I can afford it."

"Okay. I think the chicken parmesan sounds good. I'll have that with fries."

"I've had it. It's very good."

She placed the menu down on the table and Reece raised his hand when the server started to walk past the table.

"We're ready when you get a chance."

"Yes, sir. I'll be right back."

"I've never been here before," Rissa said as she glanced around. "It's nice."

"It is. Very popular too." He closed his menu, set it down, leaned back in his chair, folded his arms, and stared at her.

"What?"

"You're just as beautiful as I remember," he murmured.

The heat poured through her cheeks. She'd thought it then and thought it now, this man could make her hot with a look. God, he was so damn good-looking.

"And you're just as handsome as I remember."

A grin lifted his lips. "What else do you remember?"

She leaned forward. "Everything."

"So do I."

Their server appeared beside the table with their drinks. "What dressing would you like with your salads?"

"Rissa?"

"Ranch, please."

"I'll have the same. The lady will have the chicken parmesan with fries, and I'll have the T-bone, medium rare, with a loaded baked potato."

"Yes, sir. I'll be right back with your salads."

She toyed with her napkin. She knew he was going to try to get her in his bed tonight. What would she do? She wanted him but she also didn't want a repeat of the aftermath from Helena and seeing him all the time would just break her heart. Mentally shaking her head, Rissa decided she'd have to cross that bridge when she came to it.

Chapter Four

Reece couldn't take his eyes off her. She was so beautiful, and he was really hoping to get her into his bed later. She kept glancing around like she was nervous, and he bit back a grin.

"Why are you so nervous?"

She huffed. "I have no idea. It's not like we haven't been alone together."

"Right, but you keep looking around and ignoring me."

"You could never be ignored. There are women in here staring at you right now. It makes no difference to them that you're with me."

"Not interested in them. I'm only interested in you."

"For now."

He frowned. "Rissa, I don't know what you want me to say about that. Am I making you nervous?"

"No, not at all. I'm just wondering what I'm doing here."

"I am not going to pressure you. If it happens, it happens. If it doesn't, it doesn't." He shrugged.

"I hope you'd never pressure me. I have to be honest with you, Reece. That girl you spent the night with, in Helena, that wasn't the real me. I'd never done anything like that before and I'm not real sure I ever would again. But that one night with you was better than anything I ever shared with men who claimed to care about me. I don't want a broken heart. I've been there already so I guess I'm trying to decide if you're worth just going to bed with while hoping my heart doesn't get involved."

"If I'm worth it? Well, sweetheart, I think you are, but I don't want you to get hurt either, especially by me. I've told you how I feel about falling in love. I don't believe it can last. I guess you can say I don't believe in love, but trust me, I've seen it firsthand. Love isn't real. If you want me to drop you off at your apartment after dinner, I will. We can forget we ever met. Although, I'm not sure I can actually do that, but I promise you'll never hear from me again."

He watched her nibble on her bottom lip and he wanted to reach across the table, grab her, and kiss her senseless. To know he'd found her again, but that he can't have her was making his gut ache.

"How about we just see how it goes?"

He sucked in a breath. "Damn. Now I'll get heartburn eating too fast so we can get out of here."

When Rissa laughed low in her throat, his dick twitched. That was one sexy sound and he remembered hearing it in his ear. That night in his suite had been the hottest night of his life and even before it was over, he'd wanted more. He *never* wanted more, but he did with this beautiful woman across from him. The server appeared with their food and they dug in.

"So, what did you mean by cases? And what's with the gun?" Rissa asked him as she cut into her chicken.

"I'm an agent for the Montana Department of Livestock. I carry a badge and a gun." He shrugged.

"Is that a dangerous job? Of course, it is if you carry a gun."

"It can be very dangerous."

Her head tilted to the side. "Why were you in Helena?"

After he chewed and swallowed his bite of steak, he picked up his napkin to wipe his mouth.

"I was there on a case. I was on the trail of some rustlers—"

"Rustlers? Seriously?"

"It goes on a lot more than you think. Although the agency does more than that, that's the division I'm in."

"Did you catch them?"

"No, they managed to evade me but as soon as I locate them again and the weather clears enough to make the trip, I'll be going after them. And I'll get them."

"I believe you will."

"Damn straight. I won't give up until I do. How's your dinner?"

"It's wonderful. Your steak looks good."

"Best steaks around."

"You know what gets me…how we never crossed paths in Clifton. I mean, you came into the diner as much as anyone yet we never saw each other." Rissa shook her head.

"Well…I actually thought I saw you in there one day. Earlier this month, I think. I was sitting beside Preston and just caught you out of the corner of my eye. I jumped up and he wondered what the hell I was doing. Then I just convinced myself I must have seen Lanie or Deidra. Looking back though, I wonder how I didn't see the resemblance. Oh, and I thought I saw you going into Paige's one day."

"I did go into Paige's recently. It is strange, isn't it? The gods were against us," she said with a laugh.

Reece chuckled and nodded.

After they both finished eating, the server came by to remove their plates.

"Would you like dessert?" she asked them.

He never took his eyes off Rissa. "I believe we'll wait until we get home."

Rissa stared at him. "We'll see."

The server sighed. "Lucky girl," she muttered. "I'll be right back with your check."

He watched a slow smile lift Rissa's lips and his dick lifted with them.

"You're killing me," he said quietly.

"Oh, I don't want to do that. Trust me on that."

"Damn."

The server reappeared beside the table and smiled at him.

"The check has been taken care of, sir," she said.

"Grant?" Reece asked.

"Yes, sir, so you two can leave whenever you're ready. Have a good evening." She removed their plates and glasses then walked away.

"Who is Grant?" Rissa asked him.

"The owner of the restaurant. I had to call him to get me in, but I didn't expect him to take care of the dinners. Doesn't surprise me though. It's how he is."

"That was nice of him. Have you known him long?"

"Just about my entire life. Grant, me, Noah, Boone, Dom, and Preston went to school together." He shrugged. "He's a great guy."

"So, you just call him and get us in, huh?" Rissa asked.

"Yep." Reece chuckled. He knew she'd be surprised to hear who Grant actually was but he also knew that Grant didn't want people knowing he was the owner. Grant once had a career other than owning the restaurant and had retired from it. Other than the restaurant, he now ran a ranch in Clifton. Reece mentally shook his head. Grant had been at the top of his success, but it was his decision.

He stood and moved behind her chair, held it while she got up then he helped her into her coat, shrugged his on, then placed his hat on his head, took her hand in his, and led her out of the restaurant to his truck.

He held the door for her, helped her in, then strode around the front of the pickup, opened his door, and climbed in. Without looking at her, he started the truck, drove out of the lot, and headed to her apartment. He pulled up to the steps at the back of the diner, then strolled around to the passenger side. He opened the door, put his hand out to her, but she turned in the seat to look at him. He raised an eyebrow.

"Kiss me," she whispered.

With a grin, he cupped her face in his hands, lowered his lips to hers and kissed her long and slow. Her arms wrapped around his neck as her legs encircled his waist. He slowly lifted his lips.

"As much as I'd love to take you right now, I don't want my ass getting cold."

Rissa burst out laughing. "I'd warm it for you."

"Maybe later. Come on, sweetheart, let's get in out of the cold." He took her hand to help her out.

They climbed the steps to the door where he took the key from her, unlocked it, pushed it open then nodded for her to enter but he stayed on the stoop. She turned to look at him.

"Are you coming in?"

"I think I'll give you some time to decide what you want to do where I'm concerned. You need to make a decision and me coming in right now will not give you time to do that because if I come in, I'm going to do my damnedest to get you into bed."

She smiled at him. "You're a real gentleman, Reece."

He snorted. "I'm no gentleman. I told you I wouldn't pressure you and if I go home, I'll be keeping my word." He leaned forward, gave her a quick kiss then straightened. "Good night, Rissa. I'll call you."

Turning from her, Reece made his way down the steps, climbed into his truck, then drove home.

****

The next day, Rissa moved around the diner, refilling coffee cups. She wasn't sure when she'd hear from Reece, but she was glad he was giving her time to decide what to do about him. Was keeping things casual worth it? Was risking him breaking her heart really worth it?

He made sure she knew he was only interested in sex. He doesn't believe in love and settling down in a real relationship was not something he wanted to do. Why? What had he meant by knowing it firsthand? Had he been in love at one time and had his heart broken?

"Everyone gets their heart broken," Rissa mumbled.

"Excuse me?"

She glanced down to see Ryder Wolfe looking up at her with a frown on his handsome face and laughed.

"Just talking to myself."

"Hell, been there, but you're right. We all get our heart broken, sometimes more than once, don't we?" He grinned at her.

"Yes, but don't you think we all deserve another chance?"

"Preaching to the choir here, Rissa."

She grinned. "You got a second chance, right? You're happy with Kelsey."

"Ecstatic, but I almost messed it up. She took a chance on me and I'm glad she decided I was worth it."

Worth it. Was Reece worth it? Should she take a chance?

"You men are so damn hardheaded," she murmured then walked back behind the counter. When she turned to look at Ryder, he sat there staring at her with a frown on his face. She shrugged then entered the kitchen. The poor man probably wondered where and why that conversation took a turn.

"Hey," Deidra said as she entered the kitchen, removed her coat, and hat then hung them up on the pegs.

"I didn't think you were coming in today."

"I finished my illustrations and got bored. Preston is moving the cattle and he wouldn't let me go along." Deidra drew illustrations for several authors who wrote children's books.

"Why not?"

"Because they're moving all of them. I think he thinks I'd be in the way. It's a damn good thing I love him," Deidra said, making Rissa laugh. "I thought you were off this weekend?"

"I was, but I was bored. I hate just sitting up there in the apartment alone. I'm glad you came in though. I could use the help, and I'd love to have you go upstairs with me after my shift. I need your advice."

"Reece?"

"Yes."

"All right. Let's get these people some food."

Two hours later, she and Deidra sat on the sofa in the upstairs apartment, rubbing their feet. Their shoes sat on the floor in front of them.

"I love working in the diner but damn, some days it kills my feet," Deidra said.

"I know. I have met so many wonderful people there though."

"Definitely. I met Preston there. Well, I saw him there then met him when we went to the Feed Store. That man took my breath away the first time I saw him sitting at the counter in the diner." Deidra sighed.

Rissa laughed. "Yeah, Lanie told me you were a little shook up."

"He's sexy as hell. What can I say?"

"Not a thing. I know you love him, and he definitely loves you. Lucky girl."

"So, what's going on with Reece?"

"Nothing really. He has made it quite plain that he's not interested in a serious relationship. Even though I don't want to go back to Nolan, I do want a real relationship. I want to fall in love with a good man, someone like you and Lanie have."

"Let me tell you this, when I first met Preston, sex was all he wanted too. He'd been hurt by a woman who left him because she didn't like it here, and so was afraid that I'd leave him behind. And Trent told Lanie from the start that he wasn't staying here."

"What are you saying?"

"I'm saying, if it's meant to be, it's meant to be so if you feel Reece might be the one, shouldn't you take the chance? What if he is dead set against falling in love, but you're the one he falls for? I find it hard to believe that he won't fall in love someday anyway. And who's to say it won't be with you. Look, Rissa, I don't want you to get hurt but if you don't take a risk, you may never find love at all. You and Reece have great chemistry. You said that you have never had sex that good. Well, I never did either until Preston came along, and you know Lanie says that about Trent too. I'm a firm believer in love being a part of that. I don't think you can ever really fall in love with someone who you didn't think was great in bed."

"I thought Nolan was," Rissa muttered.

"Until?"

"Reece."

"Right. I was never really impressed with Harry either, but I thought I loved him. I didn't.

Not if going by how I feel about Preston. I'm thinking that even if Harry hadn't been married, I probably wouldn't have married him. I always had my doubts about him. I caught myself thinking, how could I marry him if he didn't thrill me in bed. I don't think I would have. I'm so glad I found out he was married because I came here and met the love of my life, and so did Lanie. Now, I'm not saying Reece is yours, but how will you ever know if you don't go for it. I think most men feel that way about a serious relationship. They never want to settle down, give up their *freedom*...until the right woman comes along."

"It was so good with him. I can't believe how hot it was. I was sure we had chemistry but when he didn't call, I figured he didn't think so, only he never even saw where I put my number for him to call. He said he would have."

"There ya go. Hey, I went with it with Preston. I knew going in, he had no desire to settle down, but that man was too hot to ignore." Deidra held up her left hand. "Now see what's on my finger?"

"I'm so scared I'll end up hurt again. How do I trust my instincts when they've been so wrong so far? Nolan was certainly not the man I thought he was."

"I don't know what to tell you there, but I can tell you right now that Reece is an honorable man. Aunt Connie likes him and that right there should be good enough. She has a wonderful instinct for people. I can't tell you what to do but I do think if you don't go for it, you will regret it."

"You're right. It's not just about the sex. I like him. I really like him. He seems to be a good man and when he took me to dinner, I saw that he was raised right. He has good manners." Rissa shrugged. "I like him," she repeated.

"Trust that. I'm telling you if you don't see where it goes, you'll look back and always wonder."

"I'll call him then. He said he'd call but you know how that goes with guys. I want to let him know I'm willing to see him. Take it as it comes, right? If he thinks it's just for sex, that's his problem."

Deidra laughed. "Sounds like a plan. Remember, men have no clue about us women. I'd better get going. I want to go home to my man."

Rissa nodded. She watched Deidra pull on her coat, hat, and gloves then after a hug, she left. After locking the door, she headed for the bathroom to grab a quick shower, after which she'd call Reece. She just prayed all went well and her heart stayed intact.

****

Reece strode down the aisle of the barn toward the indoor corral but stopped when his cellphone buzzed. He pulled it from his pocket to see Rissa's number. Was she calling him to tell him she didn't want to see him? Damn, the idea of that didn't sit well with him at all. His gut ached just thinking about it. After taking a deep breath, he pressed the *Answer* button then put the phone to his ear.

"Hello, Rissa."

"Hi. Are you busy?"

"Not at all. I was just heading for the corral to get my horse. I decided to take a ride. What are you up to?"

"Five one," she said with laughter in her voice.

"Damn smartass."

"I'm calling to let you know that I'd love to see you again."

"Is that so?"

"Yes, unless you've changed your mind."

"I haven't, but are you sure? You know I don't intend it to go anywhere."

"Other than bed, cowboy."

He hissed in a breath. "When?"

"When do you want to get together?"

"Now, damn it."

"I'm off tomorrow."

"How about tonight then? You could come here." *Here? What the hell, Maddox? You never have women at your place.*

"I could do that."

"Good. I'll send you the address. Pack a bag. You can go home tomorrow."

"Awful assuming, aren't you?"

"Confident, darlin'. Tell me you don't want to spend the night with me, and I'll let you leave whenever you want."

"I'll pack a bag."

Reece grinned. "You don't need much. I'll see you around six."

After he hit *End,* he sent her his address in a text. He was looking forward to seeing her again. *She* was one of the hottest nights of his life and he hoped for a repeat performance.

He made his way to the corral to see Shiloh. When the big chocolate palomino saw him, he trotted to the rail, put his face against Reece's chest, and blew out a big breath. Reece rubbed his ears.

"Hey, boy. Let's go for a quick ride."

"A little cold out there for that, isn't it?" Terry Banks, his manager, asked him when he stepped up beside him.

"A little cold never hurt anyone. I just want to take him up to check the fence. Then I'll be right back. I'm having company in a few hours, so I'll make it quick."

"Company?"

"Yep."

"You ain't gonna say more, are ya?"

"Nope."

"Can't be a woman since you never have women here—" Terry stopped when Reece looked at him. "A woman? You're going to have a woman here? Holy shit." He took his hat off and scratched his head then resettled the hat.

"Will wonders never cease, huh? I'll be back in a little while." Reece opened the gate, stepped into the corral, hooked a lead on Shiloh's halter then led him out and to a stall to get him saddled.

He looked back over his shoulder and chuckled when he saw Terry standing there with his mouth hanging open. Once he had Shiloh saddled and ready, he vaulted into the saddle, spurred the horse, and rode at full speed from the barn. The cold air slapped at his face, but he didn't care. He was feeling happier than he had in a long while. Rissa had decided to see him again.

As he rode Shiloh, he thought about Rissa and frowned. Did she really understand that it couldn't go anywhere with him? He didn't want her getting hurt but if she was willing to see him, he knew he had to see her and damn the consequences.

Later, when he was back at the house, he heard a vehicle pull up and looked out the window to see Rissa sitting in her SUV and staring at the house through the windshield. He opened the kitchen door, and stepped onto the porch, closing the door behind him. She smiled when she saw him. He made his way down the steps to her vehicle while she opened the door, stepped out then opened the back door to get her suitcase. She stopped when she heard Skipper barking.

"He's harmless, I promise."

"He sounds big."

"He is but he thinks he's the size of a chihuahua."

He took the case from her then took her hand. A path had been shoveled so no snow was going to be carried inside. Not that he cared, he just wanted to get her inside, undressed, and under him. Or above him. Or against the wall. *Damn.*

Reece opened the door, and Skipper sat in the middle of the floor, wagging his big tail. He started to get up but Reece said no, and the dog stayed still. Reece knew he was dying to get to the new person.

"Oh, my God! Look at you," Rissa said as she dropped to her knees to hug the dog.

Skipper immediately began licking and wiggling with excitement.

"So much for making him behave," Reece muttered.

She looked over her shoulder at him. "He's adorable."

"Please don't tell him that, he's hard enough to live with. Let me take your coat, Rissa."

He held his hand out to help her up, she placed hers in his and stood. She removed her coat and handed it to him then she went back to rubbing Skipper's ears. Reece rolled his eyes and opened the door.

"Skip, out," he said, and the dog ran outside. He shoved the door closed then walked into the laundry room to open the pet door. "He has a pet door, but I keep him inside at night. You never know when a wild animal will come around," he said when he reentered the kitchen.

Rissa stood in the center of the room, smiling at him. "Do you plan on staying over there, Maddox?"

He grinned, folded his arms, and leaned back against the kitchen counter.

"I could ask you the same thing."

"Show me your home."

He frowned. "Well, that isn't what I was expecting."

"I'd like to see it...first."

He pushed away from the counter.

"Well, this is the kitchen. That,"—he pointed to the laundry room—"is the mudroom/laundry room, where Skipper can go in or out."

He took her hand and led her out of the kitchen.

"And the living room."

He watched as Rissa looked around, taking in the high ceiling with wooden beams, a wall full of bookshelves, the large stone fireplace, and floor to ceiling front windows. He started to lead her down the hallway but she tugged on his hand, stopping him. He raised an eyebrow.

"Kiss me, please. I've thought of your kisses for months."

He pulled her to him and took her lips in a deep, hard kiss. He thrust his tongue into her mouth and groaned when she tangled hers with his. He backed her up until she came against the wall beside the front windows. He moved his hands down along her hips then slid them around to the snap of her jeans. After unsnapping them, he slid the zipper down and moved his hand inside. Sliding his fingers along the elastic in her panties, he dipped them to the top of her curls. He grinned against her lips when he felt her stop breathing. Then he slid one finger through her slit to find her wet. He moved his lips across her cheek to her ear.

"You're wet, baby," he whispered.

"Yes," she whispered back in a breathless voice.

"I want to fuck you so bad that I ache."

"Then do it," she said as she pushed at his shoulders, making him step back, and kicked her boots off then slid her jeans down and stepped out of them.

Reece looked down, swallowed hard at seeing those black boy-cut panties then reached for his wallet in his back pocket. He removed it then a condom. He tossed the wallet to the couch where it landed on a cushion. Rissa grabbed the condom from him, unsnapped his jeans, slid the zipper down, pushed his clothes down past his ass, and slid her hand inside to wrap around his hard cock. He hissed in a breath when she squeezed him.

"Just like I remember," she whispered as she kissed his jaw.

He put both hands on her panties and ripped them off then tossed them. She quickly sheathed him. He picked her up and her legs wrapped around his waist and he knew he couldn't hold out much longer. When he thrust hard into her, they both groaned.

"Fuck, you feel so good." He took her lips in a deep kiss as he began to pound into her. Her arms surrounded his neck and her legs tightened around him.

"Please," she said against his ear when she pulled her mouth from his then took the lobe between her teeth, making him shudder. Her nails dug into his back through his shirt.

"I will, baby, I promise." He pulled out some then slammed back into her.

Sex was never this good before. Not with anyone, only when it was with her. Damn, what did that even mean? Mentally shaking his head, he knew now was not the time to analyze it, he wanted to send her over the edge then follow her.

He gripped her ass in his hands and pulled her tighter against him. Her breathing quickened and he felt her clench around his dick as she screamed his name. He groaned her name as he came. Leaning his forehead against hers, he sucked air into his lungs, feeling as if he'd just run a marathon. He let her legs down but still leaned against her.

"As good as you remember?" he asked as he pulled his jeans up and zipped them.

"No."

"*No?*" He stared into her eyes.

"Better." She smiled at him.

He huffed out a laugh. "I'll agree with that."

When Reece moved back from her, she started to slide down the wall, so he picked her up, tossed her over his shoulder then headed for his bedroom. He entered the room and dropped her onto the bed. She raised up on her elbows and looked at him.

****

"You owe me a new pair of panties." Rissa laughed up at him.

Reece grinned then walked to the dresser, opened a drawer, removed something then tossed it at her. She instinctively caught it then burst out laughing.

"You have my panties from Helena. I couldn't find them when I left that morning."

"They were on the floor. I picked up the blanket because I tripped on the damn thing, and there they were. I decided I'd keep them and hoped one day I'd be able to return them, and now I have."

"Did you really want to return them?"

"I did." He took a seat on the edge of the bed and touched her leg. "You are the only woman I have ever wanted to be with again after a one-night stand. Anytime I'd see a petite woman with dark hair, I'd look like a damn stalker following her until I saw it wasn't you."

"I was hoping you'd call me and when you didn't, I let Nolan talk me into going back to him. I was so disappointed in not seeing you again."

"So, it's my fault you went back to that jerk?"

"No, I'm not saying that. That's all on me. It was just that I was so heartbroken that you hadn't called, and he took advantage of my vulnerability."

"I would have called, darlin', if I could've. I promise you. I would have."

"I believe you." She glanced around the room to see a large chest of drawers, a dresser, and a stone fireplace. Looking to her left, she noticed another wall of windows.

"Keep looking at the windows," he said as he moved to the wall beside them.

Frowning, she did as he asked then gasped when he flipped a light switch, and there through the windows, she saw a sparkling pool with lights under the water. Steam was rising off it.

"Is it heated?"

"Yes, I swim at night quite a bit, especially when I want to clear my head. Want to go for a swim?"

"I'd love to." She sat up, scooched to the edge of the bed, unbuttoned her blouse then removed it. She heard Reece groan and turned to look at him wearing nothing but her black demi-cup bra.

"Dear God, you are pure perfection," he said as he strode to her, cupped her face in his hands, and lowered his lips to hers.

She wrapped her arms around his waist and kissed him back. His tongue entered her mouth to intertwine with hers. The man knew how to kiss, whether it was this long, soft kind, or the deep, hard ones. She loved them all. His hands moved to the front clasp of her bra, unhooked it, and slid the straps down her arms then tossed it to the floor.

After giving her one quick kiss, he entered a room that she presumed was the bathroom. A moment later, he returned with two towels

"How about that swim?" he asked her as he sat on the edge of the bed, toed his boots off, then stood to remove his jeans, boxer briefs, and shirt. She couldn't take her eyes off his body. It was just as gorgeous as she remembered. She raised her hands to her hair, removed the pins, and her hair spilled down around her shoulders. "You are so beautiful," he murmured. "Ready?"

"Yes."

Reece took her hand in his and led her to the glass doors. She tugged on his hand, making him stop and turn to look at her.

"Isn't it going to be cold out there?" She took her bottom lip between her teeth and noticed his eyes drop to watch her nibbling on her lip then he looked into her eyes and grinned.

"Only for a few seconds. Come on." He slid the door open, pulled her by the hand, stepped out onto the deck, and placed the towels on the back of a lounge chair.

"Holy shit, it's cold," she said, pulling her hand from his, she took off running for the pool and jumped in.

When she surfaced, she saw him still standing on the deck with a grin on his face.

"That wasn't a ten, but I'll give you a nine for effort," he said, then ran and dove in.

The water didn't even move when he went through it. Was there anything the man didn't do well? She gave a little squeal when he surfaced beside her. He pulled her close and she wrapped her legs around his waist and her arms around his neck. He nibbled on her neck then moved his lips to her ear and tugged on the lobe with his teeth. He raised his head when Skipper started barking from the deck.

"No, Skipper. He loves to get in here, but when it's this cold, I'd rather he didn't."

"He's such a big baby."

"I adopted him. No one wanted him because he was so big and being part Rottweiler, some people are afraid of him."

"I love all dogs. I do think Rotties are a little intimidating."

"It's just the reputation they have, along with Pit Bulls and Dobermans. Raised right, any dog can be a good dog. There are no bad dogs, just bad owners, in my opinion. If you ever met Sam's dog, Bo, you wouldn't think they're intimidating. He's a big baby. It just looks like he would tear you apart. Bo is a lover, not a fighter."

"I'd love to have a dog, but I'm not sure Ripley would like it much."

Reece chuckled. "I have a feeling she wouldn't like anyone being with you."

"She rules, so it would probably be a mistake to bring another animal in." She looked into his amazing eyes and slid her fingers through his wet hair. "Do you know when you stepped into the elevator, I thought you were the sexiest cowboy I'd ever seen."

"Aww, well, thank you, ma'am. I thought you were gorgeous. I was about to ask you if you wanted to meet for a drink when those girls stepped in."

She laughed. "You looked so uncomfortable with them."

He chuckled. "I was. I felt like a slab of beef the way they were eyeing me." He quickly kissed her lips. "I was hoping they got off on a floor before you did, so I could ask you to meet me in the bar."

"I'm glad they did, and I'm so happy that I met you for that drink."

"Me too. I want to do some laps. You can go inside if you'd like. Grab a shower, if you want."

"Okay, I'll do that." She kissed his lips then unwrapped herself from around him and swam to the end of the pool and walked up the steps. She grabbed a towel, dried off, and wrapped it around her. Rissa watched him slice through the water and marveled at how easy he made it look. The cool air made her shiver, so she pulled the towel tighter and entered the bedroom.

Chapter Five

Once inside, Rissa turned to look at him swimming the length of the pool. He'd swim under the water, push off the wall, and swim to the end closest to the house. He did the same thing when he reached that wall. She could stand here all night watching that long, lean body cut through the water.

Taking a deep breath, she entered the bathroom and gasped as she looked at the deep blue toilet, sink, and Jacuzzi tub. The large shower stall took up the entire back wall. The back of the shower was stone and glass-enclosed it on three sides, including the front. She could just picture him in there showering.

"He's going to drive me insane I just know it."

She turned to the tub, started the water, and whipped the towel off. Glancing around, she saw a hamper and tossed it in.

As she stood watching the water fill the big tub, she shivered and saw goosebumps rise on her skin. She heard the glass door to the patio slide open then looked over to see Reece enter the bathroom, rubbing his head with a towel. Her eyes skimmed down his body and she had to bite her lip to hold back a groan. When he took the towel off his head, she smiled looking at his messy hair, and her fingers itched to comb through it. He stopped and looked at her and a slow smile lifted those sexy lips.

"Hey, darlin'. I thought you'd be in the shower by now." He moved closer to her, leaned down, and kissed her.

"Maybe I was waiting on you, cowboy, and I'd rather get in this big tub with you." She frowned. "Do you know that's how I referred to you in my head? As my cowboy. Even when I told Deidra and Lanie about our night together, that's how I referred to you."

"You told them about that night?" His eyebrows shot up.

"We have no secrets."

"Hell. I hope you didn't give them every detail."

She laughed. "Enough. Oh yeah, they'll be looking at you a lot different now."

He shook his head and took her hand. "Get in, and I'll get in behind you."

Smiling at him, she stepped into the hot water, scooted forward, and he slid down into the water behind her then pulled her back to him. Reece rested his chin on her shoulder and she leaned her cheek against his when he wrapped his arms around her waist.

"Why didn't you have your badge or gun on in the elevator?"

"I was undercover. I had a CI tell me the men I was looking for were at the rodeo trying to sell bulls they'd stolen. I was asking around about buying some, but it never panned out. Those idiots can't sell those kinds of bulls to a rodeo. A bucking bull is usually a cross between a Brahma and another breed. The bulls I'm trying to get back are Angus, raised for beef. These are the kind of idiots I'm dealing with trying to apprehend."

"And you put your wallet in the safe because you didn't trust me?"

"I put it there because I didn't know you. For all I knew, you were going to rob me blind in the middle of the night."

"Well, I left my purse out."

"Yeah, in *my* room."

She giggled. "True."

His hands came up to cup her breasts. "These are perfect, you know that? I couldn't stop thinking about that night, and these beautiful breasts of yours. You drove me crazy that night."

"As you did me. I hated the thought of leaving in the morning and never seeing you again. That's why I left my number."

"You should have put it on my side of the bed."

She sat up, spun around, making the water slosh over the side of the tub, and narrowed her eyes. "Yeah, okay, I admit that but I was in a hurry and I happened to be by the dresser when I wrote it down," she snapped.

A grin lit up his face. "God, you're sexy as fuck when you're riled up."

"Fuck you, Maddox," she said and turned back around.

"I believe you did, darlin'," he said against her ear making her shiver.

Shaking her head, she laughed then leaned back against his chest again.

Later, she woke up and reached for Reece to find his side of the bed empty. Sitting up, she brushed her hair back and looked toward the glass doors, but no lights were on outside. She threw the blanket off, swung her legs over the side, and stood. She walked around to his side of the bed and picked up his T-shirt from the floor and pulled it on then left the bedroom to look for him.

Rissa entered the living room to see him sitting in a chair facing the fireplace, watching the orange and blue flames wrap around the logs, and reach up the flue. The only thing he wore was his jeans which were zipped but not snapped. He turned to look at her and their eyes met and held. She moved closer to him but stopped when he smirked.

"You're too beautiful for words, Darissa Gates." He shook his head. "The things I want to do to you and have you do to me."

"What do you want me to do, Reece?" she whispered as she looked at him sitting there, staring at her.

"Come here, Rissa, and take that shirt off."

After sucking in a deep breath, she slowly moved to stand in front of him, removed the T-shirt, and tossed it to the floor. He grinned up at her, lowered the zipper on his jeans, raised his hips, and pushed them off. His hard cock stood straight up, and she couldn't take her eyes off it.

"Reece."

He crooked his finger at her, and she moved closer to him.

"Get a condom from my wallet then come here and ride me."

She picked up his jeans, removed his wallet, opened it, and removed a condom. She was getting hotter by the minute. Looking him in the eye, she smiled and ripped open the packet to take the condom out. Before rolling it down over his engorged cock, she leaned down and took the head in her mouth and sucked. He groaned.

"Not now, please ride me," Reece begged through clenched teeth.

After rolling the condom on, she placed her knees on each side of him then slowly lowered herself onto him. She watched as he gritted his teeth and his hands went to her hips. She reached behind her and cupped his balls, making him groan, then she raised herself up and down along his length. She watched his face and almost came when he leaned his head back, closed his eyes, took his bottom lip between his teeth, and moaned long and low in his throat.

"I'm close," he murmured. "This is what you do to me, Rissa."

She felt his balls draw up and knew he was on the edge.

"Yes, you are close, Reece."

"Kiss me, Rissa. Now."

She leaned over him, took his lips in a deep kiss, and gasped when he moved his thumb against her clitoris, throwing her over the edge. She moaned into his mouth as a low guttural sound tore from him as he came. She lifted her lips from his. His breath was raspy as he drew air into his lungs. He opened his eyes and looked at her.

"Stand up, Rissa," he said.

"Now what, Reece?"

He got to his feet, pulled on his jeans, picked her up, and carried her to the bathroom where he turned the shower on, disposed of the condom, then they both stepped in. Reece picked up the soap and washed her then himself. He dried them then led her to the bedroom. He took a seat on the floor in front of the chair next to the bed

"Move over me. Spread your legs over my shoulders."

Biting her lip, she moved over him, and he dropped his head back against the seat of the chair. His hands grabbed her ass and he pulled her down over his face. When his tongue touched her clitoris, her gasp filled the room. She placed her hands on the arms of the chair and held herself above him. He moved his tongue along her slit, and back to her clitoris over and over. When he sucked on it, her legs started shaking, and her orgasm hit her hard. She cried out his name and burst into a million pieces. He helped her slide down his chest, and she rested her face in the crook of his neck. They laughed when Skipper huffed from where he lay on the floor.

"I forgot about Skipper." She laughed then sobered. "Oh, my God, Reece. That was so hot."

"Yeah, it was. Now we both need to get some sleep."

"In a minute," she said as she moved down his legs then looked into his eyes. "I think you need something done with this first." She wrapped her hand around his hard cock.

"You don't have to—" He hissed in a breath when she put her mouth down over him and sucked.

His hands thrust into her hair as she licked his long length then put her mouth over him again. She wrapped her hand around his cock and pumped as she ran her tongue over him. His groans were setting her on fire. His hands tightened in her hair when she slipped her mouth over him again and sucked hard. She knew he was close.

"Rissa," he moaned. "You have to stop."

Ignoring him, she pumped harder and faster, then she felt him harden even more and he came in her mouth. Sitting up, she looked at him to see him staring at her.

"Are you all right?" she said.

"Yes, that was fantastic, thank you. You didn't have to do that."

"I wanted to. I love tasting every inch of you, Reece Maddox."

"I love doing the same to you. Help me up. Let's get to bed."

"Why were you up anyway?"

"Couldn't sleep. I'm glad you got up though," he said with a grin.

"Oh, me too. Come on, cowboy, let's get in bed and get some sleep."

"All right. As much as I hate it, you have to go home later today."

She looked at the clock to see it was one in the morning. She placed her hands on his shoulders then got to her feet. When Reece held up his hand, she took it and helped him up.

Later, she lay beside him with her arm across his waist and listened to him sleeping. His deep breathing told her he was sound asleep. Though she thought she'd fall asleep easily enough, she couldn't. What was going to happen once she did go home? She knew she wanted to see him again. Was he going to be done with her or would they get together again? Was this just another one-night stand?

"I can hear the wheels turning," Reece murmured.

"I didn't mean to wake you."

"What's wrong?"

"Was tonight a one-time thing?"

"I sure as hell hope not. Do you?"

"No. I just wasn't sure. I want to keep seeing you, Reece, but I also know how you feel about relationships."

"How about we just quit worrying about it? No sense in that, is there?"

"No, I suppose not." Rissa snuggled against him, sighed when his arms wrapped around her and fell asleep.

****

The next weekend, Reece led Rissa into the barn to pick out a horse. They were going to ride up into the north pasture. Since there had been a reprieve in the weather, they decided to spend the weekend together.

As they walked down the aisle of the barn, he came to a halt when he saw Terry walking his way. He glanced at Rissa.

"This oughta be good," he murmured.

"What?"

He looked at her and grinned. She frowned up at him.

"Terry," he said.

"Hey, boss," Terry said as his eyes shifted to Rissa.

"Rissa, this is my ranch manager, Terry Banks. Terry, this is Rissa Gates."

"Ma'am," Terry said as he touched the brim of his hat then glanced at Reece again.

"It's nice to meet you, Terry." Rissa stuck her hand out to him, and he took it.

"We're going horseback riding. We won't be long," Reece told him.

"Okay." The man kept glancing between him and Rissa.

Reece did all he could not to laugh. He knew Terry was wondering what the hell was going on with him. This was the second weekend Rissa had stayed with him and Terry knew that was not the norm for him. Hell, he was wondering what was happening as well. Might be a first for him.

"I'll see you later, Terry." Reece tugged Rissa's hand and led her down to the stalls.

"Have a nice day, Terry," Rissa said over her shoulder.

"Uh, yes, ma'am...you too."

Reece chuckled when he heard Terry muttering under his breath as he walked away.

"What was that all about?" Rissa asked him.

"Terry knows I never bring a woman here. I told him about you coming out last weekend and now you're here again. I'm sure he's very confused."

"Oh, so I'm the first woman you've ever brought here?"

"Yes, ma'am. Come on, pick out a horse."

After saddling a horse for her, he led Shiloh out of a stall and heard Rissa gasp.

"He is so gorgeous," she said.

"Yes and spoiled rotten."

"He's a chocolate palomino, isn't he?"

He was impressed that she knew that. Not many people knew that palominos could be so dark, but she probably knew her horses since he knew she was a barrel racer.

"Yes."

"They're rare. That white mane just stands out. How old is he?"

"Six. I've had him since he was three. He's seventeen hands so he's perfect for my height."

"I love Quarter horses, and Morgans too."

"Holt James raises Morgans. He has some beautiful horses." He watched as Rissa rubbed Shiloh's nose and the horse seemed to love it.

Later, as they road through the north pasture, he glanced over at her. She sat a horse very well, but then she'd have to since she was a barrel racer.

"Are you still going to barrel race?" he asked.

"I doubt it."

"How long had you been doing it?"

"Ten years. I loved it. Nolan hated it. He made me quit when we lived together."

Reece reached over to grab the reins on her horse.

"Excuse me? *Made* you quit?"

"He hated me going to the competitions. He accused me of flirting with all the cowboys and said he didn't want me doing it anymore. It was him or the rodeo, and like a fool, I picked him."

"How did you go to the competition in Helena then?"

"We had a huge fight the night before when I told him I was going to ride for Jenna in Helena. I snuck out while he slept, and I left him a note and told him I was going to the competition and I wouldn't be coming back to him."

"But yet, you did."

"Yes, I did. I was lonely. I told you that. I hate being alone and I was so hoping you called." She shrugged. "Only you didn't," she snapped in response.

"For Christ's sake, Rissa. I won't take the blame for you going back to him," he said through clenched teeth.

"I don't expect you to. I blame myself, Reece. I knew it was wrong, but I did it anyway. No one can tell me how wrong it was more than I've told myself." She shook her head. "I thought we had chemistry and hoped you would call. Even after I went back to Nolan, I hoped you'd call," she repeated.

"I didn't see your fucking number," he shouted.

"Yeah, we've been over this. I was a fool to go back to him, you didn't see the number but I didn't know that. I thought you decided not to call because all you wanted was that one-night stand."

"I did, but like I said, I was going to ask for your number." He could feel his temper rising and he knew not to let it.

"Holy hell, Reece! How would I know that? I am not going to argue with you over this. Not now. Not ever again." She turned her horse around, spurred it, and headed back to the barn.

"Son of a bitch," he muttered as he kneed Shiloh to run after her.

As he entered the barn behind her, he watched her dismount then lead the horse through the barn to cool it down. He swung his leg over the horse's head, jumped down then led the horse behind him. This damn woman was going to be the death of him. He bit back a grin. Damn, she was sexy when she was pissed. When she turned the horse to head in his direction, she started past him, but he reached out and grabbed the reins.

"What?" she growled.

He tipped his head down so she wouldn't see his smile then raised it to look at her.

"I won't ask about him anymore."

She blew a breath out. "Reece, no one feels worse about me going back to him than I do. I never should have, but I did and that's not your fault. I let him persuade me because I hate being alone. At the time, Lanie had Brett, and Deidra had Harry. I wanted someone too. It was the worst mistake of my life, but it won't happen again."

Reece cupped her cheek in his gloved hand.

"Isn't the situation the same now? I mean your sisters are both in relationships and you're not. You sure you won't return with him to New Mexico?"

"No. No matter what happens between you and me, I will never go back to him. He...he scares me."

"What do you mean?"

****

Rissa took a deep breath and told him what Nolan had done to her in the past. The muscle twitching in his cheek told her how angry Reece was. She cupped his face in her mitten-covered hands.

"It's all right. He'll never get the chance again."

"If I hated him before, it is nothing to how I feel right now. I want to kick his ass."

"That would be hard to do. Like I told you, he knows karate."

Reece snorted. "Like I give a damn. If I ever get close enough, he's going down. No man has a right to do that to a woman." He leaned down, pressed his lips to hers, and pulled her tight against him. "Let's head in."

"Sounds good. I'm cold," she murmured against his lips and felt them rise in a grin.

"I know how to warm you."

"You sure do, cowboy."

Reece pulled the two-way radio from the inside pocket of his coat, called one of his ranch hands to cool down the horses, then took her hand and led her to the house. They entered the kitchen, took off their coats, hats, and gloves then hung them up. She stared up at him and smiled then laughed when he picked her up, tossed her over his shoulder, and carried her to the bedroom. He strode to the bed, placed her in the middle of it then stood staring down at her.

"Are you just going to stand there, Maddox?" she asked as she gazed up at him.

"You're so beautiful," he said in a low tone of voice. He turned and sat on the bed, toed off his boots, tugged his T-shirt up and off over his head then stood and unsnapped his jeans.

As she watched him lower them, she moaned looking at his fine ass in those black boxer briefs. She quickly shed her clothes, except for her panties and bra. She loved letting him take those off.

He turned to look at her and she saw him swallow hard then he shucked his boxer briefs and his hard cock jutted out. Licking her lips, she got to her knees, leaned down, and took just the head into her mouth. His moans turned her on and his hands fisted in her hair.

"Rissa," he whispered.

She slid her mouth down over him, but he pushed her to her back. She stared up at him. He leaned over her, pressed his lips to hers as he unhooked the clasp of her bra, lowered the straps, and had her sit up so he could remove it. After tossing it, he straightened up, hooked his fingers into the elastic of her panties, and slowly pulled them down her legs. She laughed when he threw them. He moved to the nightstand, opened the drawer and retrieved a condom. She watched as he opened the packet, took the condom out, and rolled it down over his cock. She was getting so hot she was sure she'd orgasm as soon as he entered her.

"Reece, please," she begged.

"In a minute, darlin'." He leaned down, kissed her curls then ran his tongue along her slit to her clitoris until she was on the edge, but he didn't let her fall over.

"Please," she pleaded with him.

He straightened up, grabbed her legs, and tugged her to the edge of the bed then he thrust into her hard. She gasped but wrapped her legs around his waist. He kept his arms around her legs and pounded into her.

"Ready, baby?" he asked her.

"Yes, please."

His thumb moved to her clitoris and he rubbed it as he continued to slam into her. Her belly started to flutter, and she knew she was going to come.

"I can feel you clenching around my cock, Rissa."

She screamed as her orgasm ripped through her and she could feel him throbbing inside her as he came. He collapsed on the bed beside her and they both took deep breaths. Rissa rolled to her side, placed her arm across his waist, and smiled when he wrapped his arms around her and tugged her close.

****

The following Tuesday, Reece made his way down the aisle of the barn toward his office when his cellphone buzzed. Stopping, he pulled it from inside his coat pocket and looked at the screen to see his boss's number.

"Hey, Dave," he said in the way of an answer.

"I've put Shaun on the Hartland case. I want you to get your ass to Libby. It's been going on long enough. The owner of those bulls wants them back. You need to catch those rustlers, understand? Nevada's CI told him where they were."

Damn! "Yes, sir."

"Good, get a flight out or drive but get there. No snow is predicted until next week."

"Yes, sir," Reece muttered.

"All right. Call me when you get there."

"I will." Reece hit *End* and wanted to throw his phone. He and Rissa made plans to go out to dinner tomorrow night. Taking a deep breath, he called her.

"Hey," she said when she answered.

"I have to cancel dinner, Rissa. I have a case I have to get on."

"The one in Hartland?"

"No, the one in Libby with the bulls. I'm sorry."

"It's fine. We'll get together when you get back."

"Sounds good to me. I'll call you when I get home."

"Please, be careful."

He grinned. "Yes, ma'am. I'll make it up to you."

"Damn right you will, Maddox." She disconnected the call.

Reece couldn't keep the smile off his face as he put the phone back into his pocket and headed for the house to pack. He frowned as he thought about getting back to her as soon as he could. He didn't want to feel this. Not with her. Not with any woman. His parents went through marriages like water and he didn't want to end up like that, but he hated even thinking about being with another woman because it was different with Rissa. Everything about being with her was different, even the sex was hotter with Rissa and he knew no other could compare. They'd been seeing each other for over three weeks now, probably longer than he'd ever seen any woman, but he couldn't seem to stay away.

The next morning, he made his way to the airport. After parking his truck in the lot, he climbed out, locked it then headed inside to board the plane. It wasn't a big airport, but it was crowded today for some reason.

He carried only a duffle bag, walked to the counter, and handed his ticket to the agent. She took it from him and gave him a smile, which he returned. He set his bag on the counter.

"Enjoy your flight," she said as she stared at him.

"Yes, ma'am, thank you." He reached for his boarding pass, but she held onto it. He quirked an eyebrow at her.

"Look me up if you come back through this way." She winked, let go of his boarding pass, put his duffle bag on the conveyor belt, and moved on to the next passenger.

Reece shook his head, turned, and sauntered through the terminal to find his gate. He pulled his phone out from his back pocket and took a seat. He sent a text to his boss to let him know he was boarding soon. After getting a text back, he pushed to his feet, put the cellphone back into his pocket, and resumed his seat. Stretching his long legs out in front of him, he clasped his hands across his stomach and crossed his ankles. When his flight was called, he got up and made his way to the boarding gate. Walking onto the plane, he found his seat, removed his hat, and sat down by the window. An older man took the seat next to him, gave him a nod, buckled up then opened a book.

Once the plane was in the air, Reece stared out at the clouds and thought about Rissa. This past weekend with her had been amazing. It even beat the night they spent together in Helena and he never would have thought that possible. It had surprised him that he had been so disappointed when he found her gone the next morning. He'd been hoping she'd stick around, and they'd spend a little more time between the sheets before they had to check out. Had he tried, he could have found out her name, where she lived, and six months wouldn't have been lost. Damn, it had been so hot between them, but the room had been empty when he came out of the bathroom. He had been so mad that she was gone. He dressed, packed as fast as he could then picked up his duffle bag, and left. As he rode the elevator down to the lobby, he had hoped she'd still be there, but she was nowhere to be found. He drove back to Clifton pissed off at the world thinking he would never see her again.

"But now you found her," he mumbled.

"Excuse me?" the man beside him asked.

"Nothing. Sorry, just talking to myself."

The man chuckled. "Must be a woman on your mind."

"Hell, is there anything else that makes a man talk to himself?"

"Not that I'm aware. I was married for fifty years before my wife passed away and I swear, I talked more to myself than I did to her."

Reece grinned. "I can believe it. I am sorry for your loss though."

"I miss her every day, but it's been almost ten years now. My kids keep telling me to find another woman, but Patty was the only one for me. I'm eighty years old and happy. I know I'll see her again. What about you? You married?"

"No. Never wanted to get married. My parents have been married eight times between the two of them. They've kind of jaded me on marriage."

"Aww, son, don't let them do that to you. A good woman will change your mind and your world. They do exist. I was married to one." The man turned in his seat to look at him. "So, if you're not interested in marriage, who is she that has you muttering to yourself? If you don't mind my asking."

"A woman I met on a trip to Helena over the summer. We...spent some time together and at the time, I didn't get her number."

The man laughed. "Sounds like she made quite an impression. Must mean something. What do you mean—at the time?"

Reece shook his head. "Come to find out recently, she's in Clifton and we got together again. Only I'm just not the settling down kind. At least, I don't think I am."

"Are all your friends single too?"

"No, a lot of them are married or engaged. There are a few yet who haven't settled down, but the ones who are involved with someone seem happy. My best friend recently got engaged. He was married before, but she was a damn gold digger. Then he met a woman who changed everything for him and fell hard. Fought it all the way too." Reece chuckled. "Thing is, the woman I met in Helena, the one I can't stop thinking about, she's the sister of my friend's fiancée."

"Small world. Well, if your friends are happy, maybe you shouldn't fight it so hard."

"I don't know. A lifetime of misgivings, I guess. My brother is the same way. He was engaged, but she chose a career over him and left him heartbroken."

"Well, I've never regretted a day spent with my wife. Marriage isn't always easy but if you've got the right person at your side, it's worth it. I hope you both find what you're looking for and you're happy. I'm a firm believer in everything happens for a reason. We might not understand it at the time but eventually, we do."

"Yes, sir." He doubted it because he wasn't looking for anything, but Rissa wouldn't stay out of his head. "Damn," he whispered then grinned when the older man chuckled.

Thirty minutes later, the plane landed in Kalispell, Montana. He needed to rent a vehicle then check in with another agent. The older man stood, stuck his hand out to him, and he took it.

"Good luck, son." He winked then turned and moved down the aisle of the plane.

"It was nice talking with you, sir." Reece slapped his hat on his head, moved down the aisle, and disembarked the plane.

After picking up his duffle bag, he took a taxi to head for the car rental location. He could have driven to Libby, but the flight was much quicker, and he wasn't sure how bad the roads would be along the way. Entering the rental office, he stepped up to the counter, and when the woman behind the counter looked up at him, she did a double-take. Reece wasn't vain. Never had been, but he got this reaction all the time. So did his brother, Cord, but both were humble men. He smiled at the woman.

"May I help you?" she asked him, in what sounded like a hopeful voice.

"Yes, ma'am. I need to rent something four-wheel-drive—preferably a pickup truck or SUV."

"We have a Chevy Silverado," she told him as she looked at the computer.

"That'll do." He reached for his wallet, took out his driver's license and credit card, and handed them to her. The agency would reimburse him.

"Thank you, Mister...Maddox." She continued to stare at his license until he cleared his throat. "Oh, sorry. I was just looking at...where you're from. I've been to Clifton several times." She gave him a sly smile, making him chuckle.

"It's a great town. I've lived there all my life."

"And is there a Mrs. Maddox?"

"No, ma'am. Confirmed bachelor." He leaned his forearm on the counter and stared at her. She was a beautiful redhead, but he preferred...brunettes. Petite brunettes. *Shit!* He straightened up quickly. "Could I get the keys, please? I'm in a hurry. I have a meeting I need to get to."

"Uh, sure." She moved to the computer to enter his information, but she kept glancing at him. She was probably wondering why he suddenly quit flirting with her. She printed out the forms, placed them in front of him to sign, and then handed him the keys.

"Thank you," he said, feeling like an ass.

"You're welcome. Enjoy your time in Kalispell."

"Yes, ma'am." He walked outside and headed for the dark blue Silverado. "That petite brunette is going to drive me insane, and I am not one bit happy about it," he muttered under his breath.

Aiming the fob at the truck, he pushed the button, making the horn blow, and the lights flash. Opening the back, he set his duffle bag inside on the backseat. He unzipped it and removed his weapon and holster. Slipping his coat off, he hung it over the front seat then put the belt around his waist, placed the Sig Saur P226 in the sheath, snapped the retention strap closed then pulled on a bulletproof vest with Livestock Agent stitched on the front and back. He closed up his duffle, grabbed his coat, and shrugged it on before shutting the back door. He climbed in behind the wheel, started up the engine, and shivered when frigid air blew from the vents.

"Shit, that's cold." His breath formed a cloud in front of him and fogged up the window. Reaching over, he switched off the fan then pulled out of the parking lot, hoping the heat would soon blow warmer air. "You had to travel in February. No wonder it's so cold."

Driving down the two-lane blacktop, he swore when he saw flurries. It had better not amount to much because he had to get these rustlers, and he had to do it soon. As he followed the directions on the GPS, after the hour and a half drive to Libby, he slowed to turn onto a dirt road. He crept along. This had to be where he was meeting the other agent. He stopped the truck behind a large boulder when he saw a dilapidated cabin sitting down in a valley.

Ten minutes later, he glanced in the rearview mirror to see a truck pulling in behind him. He unsnapped the button on his holster and placed his hand over the butt of the gun then sighed when he saw a man step out of the truck with a badge pinned to his coat. Reece pushed the door open and stepped out then waited for the man to get to him. He grinned when he saw who it was.

"Hey, Reece," the man said with a grin.

"Nevada, how the hell are you?" Reece stuck his hand out.

"Good. You?" Nevada Shelton placed his hand in Reece's, and they shook. "They're at an abandoned property. Come with me. I'll show you. It's not this cabin," Nevada told him.

Reece followed him around the boulder, down a path, to a group of trees until Nevada squatted down.

"I hear you've been after them for a while now."

"Too damn long. I thought I had them in Helena, but I think they found out an agent was after them and they bolted. My informant had told me they were in Helena at the time. There are four of them."

"More men should be here soon but there was an accident on the highway so they could be a while. What do you want to do? It's your case." Nevada looked over his shoulder at him.

Reece huffed. He hated waiting. "I hate to wait much longer. I have a feeling they're going to kill the bulls and hightail it out of here. I'm surprised they haven't yet."

"Probably still holding out thinking someone will buy them. I was surprised when my CI called me about them even though it wasn't my case. I guess mine and yours move in the same circle."

"I'm glad he told you. Got your vest on?"

"Sure do," Nevada confirmed.

They both scooted back then stood and made their way back to the trucks. Reece watched as Nevada opened the back door on the truck he'd arrived in and reached behind the seat. When he straightened up, Reece saw the Remington

700P, a high-powered rifle with a scope. He watched Nevada load shells into it, then gave Reece a nod.

"I've been looking around since I found out they were here and there's a path over there we can use to get closer."

"Sounds good to me, Nevada. Let's get these bastards."

With his weapon drawn, he took a deep breath and followed Nevada to the path then both men slowly made their way down until they stopped at a huge bolder and stayed behind it. Another cabin, not in much better shape than the first one, sat in tall grass with a corral beside it. Smoke poured from the stone chimney. In the corral were the bulls the rustlers had stolen.

"There's a man coming out of the house with a rifle," Nevada whispered.

"He's going to kill those bulls," Reece whispered back.

"Can't let that happen. How do you want to handle this?"

He kept his eyes on the man walking toward the animals then made a gesture for Nevada to hand him the rifle. He looked through the scope. The man had a determined look on his face, and he knew he *was* planning to kill the bulls.

"I'm going to shoot at the dirt in front of his feet and make him stop. Then I'll call out to him."

"I know you're a good shot, so go for it."

"Yeah, I *am* a good shot." He grinned then moved out from the boulder and got on one knee. He raised the rifle, looked through the scope, and fired a shot that hit the ground about two feet in front of the man, making him suddenly stop and glance around.

"Montana Department of Livestock. Put your hands up. You're surrounded."

Reece watched the man and knew he wasn't going to go quietly.

"Son of a bitch," he muttered right before the man raised his rifle and shot in his direction. The bullet slammed into the boulder, making him and Nevada duck behind it.

"Shit," Nevada said.

"You all right?" He handed him his rifle.

"Yeah, but that was damn close. Gotta love this job."

Reece grinned. "That I do."

Slowly looking around the boulder, he saw that the man had disappeared and had most likely returned inside the cabin. He wasn't sure that the old building was going to be much protection since he could see holes in the old boards of the structure. His cellphone vibrated, and he pulled it from his pocket.

"Maddox."

"Where are you? I'm here at the pickups," a male voice said.

"Hey, Ricco, about time you got your ass here." Reece grinned.

"Glad to make it. Two other agents are here with me."

"There's a path to the right of the trucks. Me and Nevada are down that path, behind a boulder. The rustlers know we're here and just fired at us. See if you guys can get down anywhere to the left of the trucks. I told them they were surrounded, so if you can let them know you're here, I'd appreciate it."

"Got it. We'll head down there—" Ricco stopped when shots rang out. "Damn it. We're heading there."

Reece didn't say more. He knew the men would get into position to get a look at the house. There were five agents now—much better odds. Looking at the cabin, he could see the rustlers moving around inside the dilapidated building. He saw the sun glint off the barrel of a rifle as it slid out from the slats and he moved back just in time as they shot in his direction.

"I don't think they're going to go quietly," Nevada murmured.

"Doesn't look like it." Reece shot back and watched as wood particles flew off the house where the bullet struck. He had a feeling this wasn't going to go well, and he always trusted his gut. More shots rang out from the cabin and the agents fired back. He hissed in a breath when a bullet grazed his arm.

"You okay?" Nevada asked him.

"Just a graze. Not the first time, and it probably won't be the last." He aimed and fired.

After a few minutes of shooting, one man yelled they were coming out.

"Lay your weapons down and step out with your hands in the air, then get on your knees," Reece called out.

His arm was on fire. The pain was almost bringing him to his knees. He looked down to see a hole in his coat, making him swear as he saw blood oozing out and spreading across the cloth. He stood and removed his coat then pulled his flannel shirt aside to see that it hadn't been a graze at all, he'd been shot.

"Son of a bitch," he muttered.

Nevada moved closer to him. "I thought you said you were just grazed?"

"Wishful thinking. Hurts like a bitch now that the adrenaline is wearing off."

"Do we need to call an ambulance?"

"Nah, I'll go to the hospital myself." Suddenly, Reece sat down because he was feeling woozy.

"Really? I think one of us should take you. You could pass out from loss of blood."

"Okay, you can take me but let's get these jerks arrested and hauled in first. Someone will have to drive my rental. Get those men first," he slurred his words.

"You got it. Sit down against the boulder, Reece." Nevada pulled his cellphone from his pocket, called Ricco to let him know Reece had been shot then looked at him. "I'll be right back for you, Reece."

Reece nodded and heard Nevada telling the rustlers to interlock their fingers behind their heads. He leaned against the boulder, fighting to stay conscious, and saw Ricco squat down beside him.

"Reece? Come on man, let's get you to the hospital. More agents are on the way, so they'll take care of the rustlers."

Reece looked at him and blinked a few times then shook his head.

"I'm losing a lot of blood. I think I might pass—"

Later, he woke up and blinked at the bright lights above him. He glanced around the room and knew he was in the hospital. Looking at his arm, he saw a bandage around it, and he was in a hospital gown.

"About time you woke up."

He turned his head to see Nevada getting up from a chair and then he moved closer to the bed.

"How long have I been out?"

"A few hours. You had to have surgery because it wasn't through and through. Looks like you'll be taking some vacation time."

"Damn it," he muttered, leaned his head back on the pillow, and stared at the ceiling then he looked at Nevada. "Tell me we got them all."

"We did and they sang like canaries on who the mastermind was. We got him too. Some big shot out of Billings. Of course, he denies it, but we have enough evidence to make it stick. Good job, Reece."

"We all did it. I need to get out of here and go home." He moved in the bed and the pain made him grimace.

"You'll have to talk to the doctor about that. I'll see if I can find him. He was just here a few minutes ago. Not sure you should fly though."

"I'm fine. Just a little pinch is all."

"Pinch? Yeah, okay. I'll be right back."

Reece was released the next day and made the trip home. He knew he had to take some time off to recover because he wouldn't be any good in the field but he could do any desk work from his home. Once he finally reached his driveway, he sighed at just being there. Terry had taken care of Skipper for him.

Damn, he hated the thought of being stuck at home. He loved being out there catching bad guys.

Pulling up to the back porch, he shut the truck off then made his way up the steps and entered his kitchen. Skipper came running at him. He squatted down and rubbed the dog's ear.

"Sorry, I can only rub one, buddy. My arm's stuck in this sling for a few weeks." He laughed when Skipper tried to get closer to him, knocking him off balance. Luckily, he fell more to his right than his left, where his bandaged arm hung supported in a sling. Even working from home was going to be a pain in the ass. *Shit.*

"Hey, Reece," Terry said as he opened the door and stuck his head in.

"Terry, thanks for taking care of Skip for me."

"No problem. Are you all right? Do you need anything?" Terry stepped into the kitchen and closed the door.

"I'm fine. I just need to take it easy for a while."

"Okay, but you let me know if you need anything."

"I will, Terry. Thank you."

After giving him a nod, Terry walked out, closing the door behind him. Reece made his way to the living room with Skipper on his heels.

Chapter Six

As Reece lay on the sofa later watching TV, nothing was holding his interest. He could see how this was going to go. Too much time on his hands for sure. He knew he should let Rissa know about his being shot but he didn't want her to worry. It was just his arm, but he doubted she'd see it that way. The thought of telling her just didn't sit well with him. He couldn't explain it, but women get worked up over shit like this and they didn't have the kind of relationship where she had the right to do that. Damn, that sure wouldn't get him any brownie points if she knew he thought that way. But it was the truth. Their relationship was the sex only kind and that's all it could ever be. The thought of being like his parents, and not be able to be with just one person for the rest of his life made it that way.

Aiming the remote at the TV, he hit the power button and watched as the screen faded to black. He placed the remote onto the coffee table, leaned his head back, and closed his eyes. The last night they were together had been so hot though. She was one sexy little package. He moaned as he thought back to her rolling on top of him...

"What are you doing?" he asked in a sleepy voice.

"Nothing...yet," she said then laughed when he blew out a breath.

"Yet?" He glanced over to the clock on the nightstand. "You do realize it's three-thirty in the morning, right?"

"Yep." She kissed his lips and moved her mouth across his cheek to his ear. When she took the lobe between her teeth and sucked on it, his breath hitched.

He moved his hands over her back and down to her naked ass and squeezed. The next thing he knew, she was kissing his neck, his chest, and moving lower. His dick was so hard, he ached and when her hand slid down and her fingers wrapped around him, he couldn't stop himself from arching his back. The pad of her thumb slid over the top of his hard cock and he knew she could feel the drop of moisture on the tip. She moved her mouth down his stomach and kissed his belly button, making him hold his breath, but when she suddenly kissed the inside of his thigh then moved her tongue across his balls, he hissed in a breath and almost came right then. Her soft laughter let him know she was enjoying herself.

"I didn't realize you were evil, darlin'."

"Oh, cowboy, you have no idea but the thing is, I'm only this way with you, so relax and enjoy," she said, right before she put her mouth down over his cock and sucked.

He couldn't stop grabbing fistfuls of her hair. He did his best not to pull on it, but when she licked him like a lollipop, he almost tugged on it. He dropped his hands to the sheets and clutched handfuls as she continued to suck and lick on him. He looked up at her when she sat up.

"I think I like having this hold on you, cowboy," Rissa said with a smile.

"You definitely have a hold on me, sweetheart."

She threw her head back and laughed. He reached up to cup her breasts in his hands, then he sat up and took her lips in a deep, hard kiss. He felt her hands on his shoulders, pushing him back down on the bed.

"I'm not done with you yet," she whispered.

"No?"

"Nope." With a wicked grin, she slid down again and took his dick in her hand then she started sucking on him again.

"Holy hell, I'm not going to last if you keep sucking on my dick like that," he said between clenched teeth.

"Good." She began to pump her hand along his hard length as she sucked on him. "You're almost there," she whispered, and it sent him over the edge.

He jackknifed up, groaned, and came hard. When he was spent, he fell back onto the bed and took deep breaths.

"Shit," Reece muttered as he sat up on the sofa.

He shook his head and blew out a breath. Just thinking about sex with Rissa was hot. It had never been that good with any other woman. He'd had more one-night stands than he could count, but he had wanted it to be more than one night with her and he'd never felt that way before. Now she was in his life more than any woman had ever been, and he had no idea what he was going to do about it. He did need to let her know about his injury though before someone else did. She wouldn't be happy about it either way.

As he lay back down on the sofa, he jerked when someone knocked on his door, then it opened, and he heard Cord call out for him.

"In here," he said.

"Let me get my coat and hat off then I'll be in. Do you need anything?"

"A beer."

Cord entered the room with two beers, handed one to him then took a seat in the recliner. They both twisted off the caps and put them on the coffee table.

"How are you doing?"

"Okay. I hate wearing this damn sling, but I can take it off for a little bit at a time. What brings you out here?"

"I wanted to see how you were doing and to tell you that Dad came to see me." Cord sighed. "Seems he's getting a divorce again."

"Holy hell. Why?"

"Karen found out he was having an affair."

"Son of a bitch." This was why he didn't believe in love. His parents were never happy. Especially his father. He couldn't seem to keep it in his pants. Reece took a swig of beer then looked at Cord. "Is she younger than Karen?"

"Hell, yes. He keeps up and he'll be after teenagers soon."

"Don't say shit like that. I would hope even he'd draw the line at that."

Cord chuckled. "It's nothing new, is it? No wonder we don't have any luck with women. Well, *I* don't. You just don't want a permanent one."

"Nothing but trouble," he muttered with a nod.

"Yeah," Cord murmured.

"You still love Faith, don't you?"

"Love of my life but nothing I can do about that. She won't be back and even if she did, I'd never take her back."

"Never say never, little brother."

"I know but, in this case, I have to. I wanted to marry her, Reece, and spend my life with her. Her damn career was more important."

"As I said, nothing but trouble."

"I'm surprised that Dad hasn't been by here to talk to you about his divorce."

Reece laughed. "Probably because he knows I'd go off on him. He knows how I feel about his love life."

"True. I didn't know what to say when he told me. I just shook my head. I don't understand him at all, or Mom, for that matter. You'd think after, maybe the third marriage, you'd say fuck it and stay single. I don't know why he can't be faithful."

"No clue. That's why I don't want to settle down. I don't want to be like him."

"I would have been faithful," Cord said, sounding sad.

"I didn't mean that part. I meant going through marriages like water. I wouldn't cheat. No one should."

"You got that right."

Reece didn't know what else he could say. Their parents were never happy. Even if he ever considered getting married, he'd want it to last. He'd want a woman he'd love until he took his last breath. *Shit!* Why would he even think about that? He had no desire to get married. Ever. He leaned his head back, closed his eyes, and he saw Rissa's beautiful face.

Damn. He quickly opened his eyes to get her out of his mind.

His brother stayed for an hour then left, leaving Reece alone with his thoughts. Thoughts of Rissa. Thoughts he shouldn't be having. Thoughts that pissed him off. Maybe it was time to stop seeing her...but damn, that sure didn't sit right with him either. Hell. He had no idea what to do.

****

Friday had Rissa being run ragged at the diner and her feet were killing her. She was about to head for the kitchen and take a seat for a minute when the bell over the door jingled and she blew out a frustrated breath. Turning around, she grabbed the coffee pot and headed for Preston as he took a seat at the counter.

"Hey, Preston," she said with a smile and filled his cup.

"Hi, Rissa. I didn't think you'd be here."

She frowned. "Why not?"

"Because of Reece." He scanned the menu.

Setting the coffee pot down, she stared at him.

"What about Reece?" Preston looked up at her, grimaced slightly, and she immediately knew something was wrong. "Preston?"

"Uh, he's fine, but...you should call him."

Rissa picked up the pot, put it on the warmer, and entered the kitchen. She hopped up on the stool, pulled her phone from her apron, found Reece's number, and hit *Call.*

"Hey, darlin'," he said.

"What's wrong?"

"Nothing, why?"

"Preston said I should call you. He wondered why I was here and not with you. What. Is. Wrong?" She heard him blow out a breath.

"I was kinda shot—"

"Shot!" She jumped off the stool and felt the blood drain from her face.

"Rissa, I'm fine. It was in my arm. I had surgery, and I'll heal. It's not that big of a deal."

"Not that—damn it, Reece. I'm coming out there after work. I only have an hour left."

"Okay."

"Okay? Just like that?"

"I want you to come here. I was hoping you'd stay the weekend again."

"I have to work this weekend, but I'll come out in a little while and leave tomorrow. Is that all right?"

"Yes, that's fine. I'll see you later then. Hey, would you bring me a burger, please?"

She laughed. "All right. Your usual?"

"Yes, ma'am. I'll see you in a while, sweetheart." He ended the call.

Rissa hit *End,* put the phone back into her apron pocket, and walked out to get Preston's order.

"What'll you have, Preston?"

"My usual. I'm sorry you didn't know about Reece. He's probably going to try to kick my ass now."

"*Try?*"

Preston chuckled. "Yeah, *try*. He's never been able to. Won't be different now." He shrugged.

"I don't understand why Deidra didn't tell me about Reece," she said.

"She's been really busy. She has some illustrations she needs to get finished. Otherwise, I'm sure she would have, or maybe she thought you already knew."

Nodding, she turned, looked over her shoulder when the bell jingled and saw Nolan enter. *Damn it!* Ignoring him, she headed for the kitchen to give her uncle, Preston's order.

"You never hand me orders. You always put them on the wheel. What's up?" her uncle asked her.

"Between finding out that Reece was shot and Nolan coming in, take your pick."

"I thought you knew about Reece, and I will kick McCabe out of here if you want me to. I don't like that punk."

"I know, but I don't want to make him any madder than he already is, and how would I know about Reece?"

"Hell, honey, everyone's been talking about it."

She gasped. "I did hear someone talking about someone being shot but I never thought it was Reece." She put her hands over her face. "It never occurred to me that he could be shot."

"He deals with a lot of rustlers, and some of them feel they have nothing to lose. He knows the risks." He frowned at her. "Why does that bother you so much?"

The heat rushed into her cheeks. "Uh, well..."

"Because they're seeing each other. My goodness, Owen, don't you know what goes on in your own diner?" Connie said as she entered the kitchen.

The look on her uncle's face was priceless and Rissa bit her lip to keep from laughing.

"First off, it's not *my* diner and second, I mind my own business. Unlike some others."

Connie laughed. "Gossip happens in a diner, hon."

"We've only been seeing each other a few weeks...so how does everyone know that already?" Rissa frowned.

"Because you were seen in the Hartland Restaurant. Enough said." Connie winked at her. "I think it's great, but just be careful. Reece isn't known for his relationship skills and I don't want you getting your heart broken. I will kick Reece Maddox's ass if he hurts you."

She hugged her aunt. "I'm a big girl. I can take care of myself. Haven't I proved that by telling Nolan to get lost?"

"Yes, but he is still around. I really think you should get a restraining order. Talk to Sam, please."

"All right. At least when I'm working, he won't be able to come in here. I need a burger to go for Reece. His usual."

"All right. We want you to talk to Sam though." Owen turned back to the grill.

She nibbled on her bottom lip. If she did get a restraining order, she knew it would only piss Nolan off and a piece of paper wouldn't stop him from trying to talk to her. Even if Sam arrested him for violating the order, or ran him out of town, Nolan would somehow get back to Clifton and try to see her. It was a damned if you do, damned if you don't situation. Maybe she should just talk with him because ignoring him wasn't working. If she sat him down and told him just how she really felt, he'd get the message and leave. There was no way she was going back to him, or Albuquerque, for that matter. Her family was here now. Reece was here, and she was this close to falling in love with him. She knew she was going to end up with a broken heart, but it was a risk she was willing to take. Just thinking back to that last time they were together made her hotter than standing in front of a blast furnace.

With a deep sigh, she got back to work. She picked up the coffee carafe and walked to where Nolan sat then poured him a cup of coffee.

"Darissa, please talk to me," he said in a low tone of voice.

"All right, I will, but not today. Come up to my apartment tomorrow night after six and we'll have a discussion. One I'm sure you're not going to like." She turned away from him and moved to fill some other cups. When she stepped in front of Preston, he sat there staring up at her with narrowed eyes.

"Do you seriously think that's a good idea?"

She shrugged. "I have to get it across to him that it's over."

Preston glanced at Nolan then back to her. "Maybe someone should be there with you."

"I can take care of myself. He won't hurt me."

Preston snorted. "First fucking time for everything, Rissa."

"I'll be fine."

Preston shook his head, picked up his cup, and took a sip. She walked away from him and moved through the tables to get orders. The last hour dragged on as she worked. At four, she entered the kitchen, removed her apron, shrugged on her coat, hat, and gloves then she picked up the white bag with Clifton Diner scrolled on it containing Reece's order, waved at her aunt and uncle, and started for the door. As she was about to go out, Preston appeared beside her.

"I'm walking you up," he said in a no-nonsense tone.

"Fine."

Preston chuckled. "Like hell it is. Women never say fine when it is, only when it isn't."

She laughed. "You learn quick, cowboy."

"Your sister has taught me well."

With a smile, she opened the back door and stepped outside to see snow coming down. They walked to her stairs, and Preston nodded for her to go up while he stood at the bottom. She started up the steps.

"Lock the door behind you."

"I'm going back out in a few minutes. I just need to grab a shower."

"Where the hell do you need to go tonight in this snow?"

She turned and glared at him. "I am going to see Reece, not that it's any of your business."

She watched as he tipped his head down, so his hat covered his face and she knew it was to hide a grin. When he raised his head, she could see the laughter in his eyes. Then he started up the steps.

"Yes, ma'am. I'll just wait inside then and walk you back down to your SUV."

"Preston—"

"No excuses. Move it." He jerked his chin for her to continue up the stairs.

"Hardhead," she muttered.

"You have no idea."

She unlocked the door, opened it, stepped inside, and Preston followed her. She locked the door and looked up at him. He really was gorgeous too. Her sister was a lucky woman. She set the bag on the table beside the door, along with her keys.

"Happy now?"

"God, I can tell you're Deidra's sister."

She burst out laughing. "Wait until the time comes when all three of us are with you."

"I shudder at the thought." He took a seat on the sofa. "Go do what you have to do then I'll walk you down. I just need to text Deidra and tell her I'm running a little behind."

"All right." She headed to the bathroom to shower and get the diner smell off her.

Once she finished washing her hair and herself, she quickly dried off, used the blow dryer on her hair, and dressed. After packing a small bag, she walked back into the living room to see Preston on the sofa with Ripley lying beside him. They were staring at each other.

She walked to the coat rack and set her bag down.

"I'm surprised she tolerated you on her sofa." She smiled when he quickly got to his feet. Cowboys and their manners.

"Almost as soon as I sat down, she jumped up here. I don't think she likes me."

"She's not really fond of anyone. She's a cat."

He chuckled. "True. You ready?"

"Let me get some food and water for her. Then I will be." She took care of feeding Ripley then pulled on her coat, hat, and gloves. After turning on a tableside light, she smiled at Preston and picked up her case and the bag containing Reece's burger.

"Let's go." He opened the door for her then pulled it closed once they stepped onto the stoop then he took the case from her.

She locked the door, turned to go down the stairs, and saw snow covering them and it was still falling. Preston took her hand in his and helped her down so she wouldn't fall. Some men still had manners. He walked her to her SUV and stood beside it while she unlocked it, got in, and started it. She put the window down. He opened the back door, set her bag inside then closed the door.

"Thank you, Preston. My sister is a lucky woman."

He grinned. "Damn right, she is." He tapped the top of her vehicle then stepped back. "Drive safe."

She gave him a wave, put the window up then headed for Reece's place. The roads were beginning to get covered and she hoped she was able to get back tomorrow. She wasn't working Monday, but it was her weekend to work the diner and although she loved working for her aunt and uncle, she had to admit she'd rather be with Reece.

She shook her head, thinking about him being shot and not telling her. Damn stubborn man. Why hadn't he called and told her? Did he think she would get hysterical? Well, she might have had a moment of small panic when she heard about it but if he was all right, she was fine. Still pissed though. He should have let her know. She wrapped her hands tight around the steering wheel and told herself to calm down. Maybe he didn't think she needed to know because they weren't in a relationship. The idea of that just made her stomach ache. She wanted to be with him and not just for sex. She knew going into this, a relationship with Reece Maddox was an impossibility. That it wouldn't happen. He didn't want to settle down. He was against falling in love. Perhaps it would be easier to understand if only she knew what his problem was.

Pulling into his driveway, she drove up to the side of the house, parked her vehicle and stepped out then removed her suitcase from the back. The temperature had dropped since the sun had set. Winter seemed to be hanging on in Montana this year. Of course, her aunt had told her it could snow as late as April and as early as September. Considering it was just February, the snow was expected. She blew out a breath and watched it form into a puffy cloud. She walked up the steps, stomped her booted feet to remove snow, knocked then opened the door. Skipper sat at the door staring at her. The dog was as intimidating as hell, but she knew it was only a façade. She set her suitcase on the floor.

"Hi, Skipper," she whispered.

She set the paper bag on the counter then reached down to rub his ears. His tail wagged and she huffed a relieved sigh. Turning from him, she pulled off her hat, mittens, and coat then hung them on the peg by the back door. She smoothed her hand over her hair because she could feel the static and she was sure it was sticking straight up.

"Hi."

She spun around to see Reece leaning against the doorjamb with his left arm in a sling. She bit her lip to keep from crying. She moved to where he stood, stopped in front of him, and gazed into his face. He was just so devastatingly handsome.

"Are you all right?" Rissa lightly touched the sling.

"I'm fine. Just a little sore."

She placed her hands on her hips. "Why didn't you tell me about this, Reece?"

He shrugged. "It wasn't a secret. I'm sure all of Clifton was talking about it. I figured you'd hear about it."

"You figured—damn it, Reece. I didn't until today, and you had surgery days ago. Didn't you think I deserved to know?"

"Deserved to know? I really didn't think about it. I was going to tell you but just forgot."

She stared at him and her jaw dropped. She snapped it shut and narrowed her eyes.

"Well, that certainly puts me in my place, doesn't it?"

"Rissa, you are making this out to be more than it is."

"What? Your injury or us?"

"Probably both." Reece shrugged.

She gasped as pain ripped through her. "At least you're honest."

She turned around, walked to her coat, pulled it off the peg, opened the door, picked up her suitcase, and looked back at him.

"I hope you get better soon. Goodbye, Reece. Oh, your burger is in the bag on the counter. You know what you can do with it." She was about to close the door when his voice stopped her.

"You knew this going in. I made it clear from the start that I wasn't into relationships. I never have been. I have been honest from the beginning and you agreed to it."

"Yeah, I did. Forgive me for not remembering that." Rissa walked out and slammed the door behind her. She didn't even put her coat on as she opened the back door, set her case inside then climbed into her SUV, started it, and tore out of there to head home.

****

"Son of a bitch," Reece roared and winced when the door slammed.

He should have just kept his damn mouth shut. He liked being with her. Hell, he liked her. Way more than he should but he just didn't want to get in a relationship. Love does not last. At least, not in his family. His father went

145

through women like people go through underwear and his mother wasn't much better. His brother was still nursing a broken heart after three years. Cord had been torn apart when Faith left him, but Reece believed he was finally on the mend.

Love never lasts. It had been his mantra for a long time. Rissa knew going in, damn it. Shit. He was going to miss being with her. They just about set the sheets on fire, and it wasn't easy getting enough of her. Hell. What the hell was he supposed to do now? His phone buzzed and he picked it up to see Preston's number.

"Hey, Preston."

"Did Rissa make it there?"

"Uh, yeah. Why?"

"Because I walked her to her SUV, and it was really beginning to snow, so I was just checking on her. Can Deidra talk to her?"

"She's not here."

"You just said she made it there," Preston snapped.

"She did, damn it, and now she's gone," Reece practically growled.

"What the fuck did you do, Reece? I'll gladly make a trip out there and kick your ass."

"Fuck you, Mitchell." Reece hit *End* on his phone and drew his arm back to throw it then thought better of it.

He practically marched to the living room and flopped down onto the sofa. Why had he started this shit with her? He never did that. It was always a one-night stand and move on. Hell, since having her that night in

Helena, he had even followed women who looked like her from the back until they turned, and he knew for sure it wasn't her. No woman had ever stuck in his head after he was done with her and made him feel like he wanted to see her again. None of them...until Rissa.

Bringing women to his home never happened either, yet he had Rissa spend the night with him. What the ever-loving fuck? He wasn't looking for Miss Right, just Miss Right Now. It was the way it always had been and then some petite brunette comes along, and he can't stay away. He couldn't keep his hands off her and he knew when he looked at her in the elevator, he wanted her for more than one night.

"Son of a bitch," he muttered.

Reece did not need this shit. Women were nothing but trouble, but Rissa was different. She was so damn hot, in and out of bed. She was so beautiful with her green eyes, dark hair, and God help him, her body. She was perfect. Her breasts fit right in his hands. Closing his eyes, he could see them with their rosy-hued nipples. Christ, now his cock was twitching. All he had to do was picture her in his mind and he went rock hard. The things she could do with those sexy Cupid's bow lips. He groaned and sat up. Placing his elbow on his thigh, he rubbed his hand over his head. What the hell was he going to do?

****

Rissa pulled her SUV into the parking lot, slammed the gear into Park, leaned her head against the steering wheel, and sobbed. Damn that man! How dare he act like she had no right to be concerned? Did he think she just slept with any man who came along? She'd told him the night in his hotel room that she never did that, and he believed her—or so she'd thought. Maybe she came across as a slut that night, but she wasn't one. She didn't sleep around. That night was the first time she had ever done something that spontaneous. He had been hard to resist. As soon as he stepped into the elevator, she wanted him. She hadn't lied when she told him she thought he was the sexiest cowboy she'd ever seen. Then after they meet up again, he wants to see her...not just once but more. Now, he acted like it was no big deal to tell her he'd been shot. They might not be a couple, but common courtesy would make anyone tell someone what happened especially when they had been seeing each other.

She sat up and hit the steering wheel with her hand then swore when it hurt. Taking a deep breath, she shut the SUV off, pulled her coat from the passenger seat, got her suitcase out then made her way to the back stairs. She climbed them, inserted her key, opened the door, and stepped into the warm apartment. Ripley wound around her ankles as she set the suitcase down.

"Looks like it's just you and me, girl." She rubbed the cat's ears then straightened up. After stuffing the mittens and her beanie in the pockets, she hung the coat on the coat rack and locked the door then placed her keys on the table beside the door.

Making her way to the sofa, she plopped down, picked up the remote, aimed it at the

TV, and turned it on. As she flipped through the channels, she saw nothing that interested her. Her phone buzzed and she picked it up to see Deidra's face.

"Hey, sis."

"Rissa, what's going on? Preston said you went to Reece's, but he called to make sure you made it and Reece said you left."

"Nothing is wrong. All of that happened. We're done."

"Look, sis, I'm worried about you."

"I'm fine. Well, I will be. I should have known not to get involved with him. He warned me. I guess I expected too much."

"If Preston doesn't kick his ass, I will."

"No, Deidra. You and Preston just let it go. I don't want it to ruin their friendship. I'll be all right."

"Just promise me you will not go back to Nolan."

"You don't have to worry about that. I'm going to take a long hot bath to help me relax then I'll go to bed. I'll talk to you tomorrow. Love you."

"I love you too. I shouldn't have told you to take a chance. I'm here for you."

"It is not your fault. I knew what I was doing," Rissa whispered and hit *End.*

Pushing to her feet, she headed down the hall to the bathroom. She didn't need to take a bath, but she thought it would help the tension go away. She entered her bedroom first to undress, picked up her robe, and made her way to the bathroom. As she crossed the hall, a knock sounded at her door. Frowning, she pulled her robe on, tied the belt, and slowly made her way back to the living room and jumped back when someone pounded on the door. Then she heard Reece's voice.

"Rissa? It's me, open up," he yelled through the door.

She walked to the door, looked out the peephole, then opened it. He strode in past her and she could feel the cold coming off him. She pushed the door closed.

"What are you doing here, Reece?" She folded her arms and stared at him.

He turned to look at her. Snow covered the shoulders of his coat and the brim of his hat.

"We need to get a few things straight."

"You came all the way here? You could have called."

"And have you hang up on me? I don't think so." He removed his hat and coat then placed them on the coat rack.

"Gee, take your coat off and stay awhile," Rissa said with as much sarcasm as she could muster.

****

Reece smirked, walked to the sofa, and stood beside it. Staring at her, he knew he shouldn't have come here. It wasn't going to go well. He tried like hell to keep his eyes off her robe because he was sure there was nothing under it but her.

"Where's your sling?" Rissa asked as she sat in the overstuffed chair and curled her legs under her.

"Home. I don't need it all the time." He took a seat on the sofa.

"What things do we need to get straight? That you're a prick? Yeah, I know that."

"Damn it, Rissa. You knew going in that this was not going to go anywhere."

"I went to see you because I was worried about you. *You* turned it around so you could remind me of that."

"I just don't want you thinking—"

"For God's sake, Reece, I get it. Okay? I get it."

He stared at her then hung his head and ran his hands through his hair then fisted them.

"You are driving me crazy," he growled out. He pressed the heels of his hands against his closed eyes then pinched the bridge of his nose.

"Reece, what do you want me to say?"

He glanced over at her and narrowed his eyes.

"What do I want you to say?" He shot to his feet. "Not a fucking thing. This can't go anywhere. This is not what I want in my life. I'm too damn busy to fool with you." He winced when she hissed in a breath. "I'm sorry, but it's the truth. I told you at the beginning that I am not the settling down type. I don't want to settle down. I don't want to get married, and I don't want to have kids. What the hell do you want from me?"

"Obviously, nothing from *you* because I want *all* of that. You could at least tell me why you don't want any of that."

He blew out a breath. "Because I've seen all the destruction it can cause. I've lived it. My parents have been married eight times between them and my dad is getting *another* fucking divorce. If I've learned anything at all, it's that love does not last. Not in my family anyway, and I will not get married and end up like them. I won't do it!"

She got to her feet, walked to the door, and opened it. "Goodbye, Reece."

He huffed out a breath, walked to the coat rack, picked up his coat and hat then walked out the door. After placing his hat on his head, he pulled his coat on then turned to say something, what, he didn't know, but he never got the chance since she shoved the door closed in his face. *Son of a bitch!* He turned to start down the steps, but he heard her crying from inside. After a slight hesitation, he took a deep breath, then trotted down the steps. It was for the best. He hated making any woman cry, but it was tearing him apart knowing Rissa was crying because of him.

Making his way to his truck, he hit the fob to see the lights flash. Out of the corner of his eye, he thought he saw someone but when he looked around, the alley was empty. He wouldn't put it past McCabe to be hanging around but why anyone would be out in this weather was beyond him.

"You're out in this weather, dumbass," Reece muttered as he opened the truck door, climbed in, and started it. The vents blew warm air. That was how quick his trip up to her apartment had been. He had no idea what he'd been thinking by coming in here to talk to her. Maybe he thought she'd tell him she was willing to see him on any terms. Then she throws out that she wants so much more than what he was willing to give. He hit the dash with his fist, put the gear into Drive, and tore off down the alley.

****

The next night, Rissa opened the door to let Nolan in. He bent down to pet Ripley, but the cat ran from him. Trying not to grin when he sighed, she closed the door and looked at him. He removed his coat and hung it on the coat rack.

"Have a seat. Would you like something to drink?"

"Do you have any coffee? This damn place never warms up," he muttered as he took a seat on the sofa. Reece would have waited until she sat or at least, sat then stood up when she entered the room again.

"I'll be right back. It will only take a minute." She watched as he tried to get Ripley to come to him without success.

"Did you turn my cat against me, Darissa?"

"She was never your cat and you know it. I adopted her, not you. I'll only be a minute."

She entered the kitchen, put the K-cup in the machine, and made him a cup. Once it spewed out, she picked it up and took it to the living room then handed it to him.

"You remembered I like it black."

"Yeah, don't get all excited about that. It's no big deal."

"Damn, Darissa. What is wrong with you? You've changed since you've been here."

"Not really. I've always spoken my mind, you just never noticed because you were rarely home. You spent all your spare time with your friends instead of me and the way you were treating me was uncalled for. I won't put up

153

with that anymore. I love it here and I want you to get it through your head that I'm staying here, Nolan. It's over between us."

"Because you're fucking that cowboy?"

She gasped. "Who I fuck is none of your business. Not anymore."

He shot to his feet and grabbed her wrist. "The hell it isn't. I want you to come back to Albuquerque with me."

She jerked her wrist from him and took several steps back. "No. I am not leaving here."

"You won't make it without me. You'll come crawling back like you did before."

"That was a mistake. One I won't repeat."

"You think he loves you? He doesn't. I know his type. He wants one thing and one thing only. You in his bed."

"I've been in his bed," she shouted.

"You bitch." Nolan put his hands against her shoulders and pushed her back against the wall and put his face close to hers. "I won't leave until you go with me."

"This is why I won't, Nolan. You like scaring me. I'm done with being intimidated by you. If you touch me again, I will report you to the sheriff. Now, get out. It's done. *We're* done."

When someone suddenly pounded on the door, he let go of her and stepped back then the door flew open and hit the wall. She looked over to see Preston coming in with Deidra behind him. Preston walked right up to Nolan and glared down at him.

"Get the fuck out of here. Now," he growled out.

Nolan walked to the coat rack, grabbed his coat, pulled it on then turned to look at her.

"It's not over until I say it is. It would be a shame if something happened to your cowboy." Nolan glanced at Preston and Deidra then back to her. "Or anyone you care about for that matter," he sneered.

"You threatening me, boy?" Preston said as he took a step forward.

Nolan scoffed at him. "If I was?"

"I'll kick your ass out of Clifton."

"Anytime you want to try. The bigger they are, the harder they fall," Nolan said then stepped outside and slammed the door behind him.

Rissa collapsed onto the sofa, shaking. She knew Nolan could hurt Reece or Preston if he really wanted to. Men like Nolan didn't care who they hurt. She'd been shocked when he pushed her against the wall but she'd told the truth, she would report him to Sam in a heartbeat. Deidra sat down beside her and wrapped her arms around her.

"Please come to the ranch with us," Deidra said.

"No, I'm fine. He won't get in unless I let him in, and I never will again." Rissa looked up at Preston. "Thank you, but please be careful. You're on his radar now. He won't hesitate to go after you or Reece."

"I'm not afraid of him and I know Reece isn't either. We're here for you anytime, Rissa," Preston said.

Rissa nodded. Reece and Preston might not be afraid of Nolan, but she knew what he could do if he put his mind to it. Why had he changed so much? No man owned a woman, but Nolan thought she was his property. One man wanted nothing of her as his and the other wanted all of her to be his. She just didn't understand men.

****

March brought even colder weather if that was possible. Reece sat at his desk at the Montana Department of Livestock office and looked over cases. Rustling was at a high level this year already and he was more than ready to get out there and catch the men doing it.

"Hey, Reece."

He glanced up to see Nevada standing in front of his desk. He slid the chair back, stood, and put his hand out to shake his hand.

"Nevada, it's good to see you again. What are you doing here?"

"I have a case."

"Good. I never got the chance to tell you that I appreciated your help on that other case."

"It was my pleasure. Good to see you in the office again. How's the arm?"

"Fine. I'm ready to get out in the field."

"Dave okay with that?"

"Haven't asked yet. I want to find a case first. I see the one from Hartland was solved."

"Yeah, Ricco got them. There's a huge case going on right now in Spring City. About a hundred head of cattle were stolen."

"Damn, I'd love in on that."

"Talk to Dave. Maybe he'll send you with me. I can't do that one alone."

"I'll talk to him now. Thanks, Nevada."

Nevada nodded. "Sure thing."

He watched as Nevada walked to a desk and took a seat then he took a deep breath and headed for the boss's office. The department wasn't big, just a few men since the headquarters were in Helena and this was just a district office in Clifton. He knocked on the glass door and saw Dave look over then wave him in.

"Reece, what can I do for you?" Dave took his glasses off, tossed them onto the desk then pinched the bridge of his nose.

"I'd like in on the case with Nevada."

Dave raised his head and stared up at him. "Is that so?"

"Yes, sir. I need to get back out there."

"Reece, you just got back from an injury. Are you sure that's wise?"

"I'm fine, Dave. I'm going insane in this office and the one at home."

Dave leaned forward and placed his arms on the desk.

"Tell you what, you get me a release from a doctor and you're in. If he says no, then you will sit your ass at a desk, and work from there. We clear?"

"Yes, sir. I'll make an appointment."

"Wait. Shouldn't you have seen him anyway?"

Reece clenched his jaw. "Yeah, well, I canceled the appointment since I felt fine."

Dave laughed. "Of course, you did. Get me a release. You would probably already have it if you weren't so damn stubborn. I don't know what you were thinking by canceling that appointment. You know damn well I won't let you go back to work without a release." He picked up his glasses, put them on, and Reece knew he'd been dismissed.

Damn it. Now he'd have to see the doctor and explain why he hadn't been in for his last appointment. He knew Dave would want a damn release. It was policy. No one could return to fieldwork after an injury unless the doctor allowed it. Damn. Heading back to his desk, he picked up the phone and made an appointment. He needed to get out in the field. Maybe then he wouldn't think about Rissa so much. He really missed her. It had been far too long since he had seen her. Anytime he went into the diner, she wasn't there, and he wasn't sure if it was because she was hiding in the kitchen or she wasn't working.

After work, he decided to head to the diner for a burger and hoped he saw her. God, he missed her. He entered the diner and people waved or called out to him. He gave them a wave and took a seat on a stool. Looking around, he saw Lanie and Deidra but not Rissa. Deidra stepped in front of him.

"What can I get you?" she asked him without actually looking at him.

Damn, talk about a cold shoulder.

"Uh, my usual is fine with coffee."

"Fine," she said, turning away.

When women used that damn *fine*, it was the ultimate *fuck you*. Sighing, he spun around on the stool and glanced about. The place was busy, but then it always was. He turned back around when a coffee cup was practically slammed onto the counter and he looked up to see Lanie pouring him a cup and looking like she wanted to pour it over his head.

"Hello, Lanie."

"Hello," she said then walked away. Son of a bitch. The Gates' women were tough.

A few minutes later, Deidra set his burger down in front of him and turned to leave.

"Deidra?" She looked over her shoulder at him. "Where's Rissa?"

Deidra snorted. "Like I'd tell you. Enjoy your dinner."

"Ouch," a voice said from beside him and he glanced to his right to see Jim Barton taking a seat.

"All three of them are pissed at me."

Jim laughed. "I kind of figured that. It's bad enough having one woman pissed at ya, but three." He shook his head. "Damn, son, you screwed up."

"You have no idea." Reece picked up his burger, took a bite, chewed, and swallowed. He'd lost his appetite. He picked up his coffee and took a sip. Connie appeared in front of him and refilled his cup. He looked up at her to see her glaring at him then she walked away. "Shit. Make that four."

Jim Barton burst out laughing as he picked up his coffee cup to take a sip.

"Better you than me, boy. Better you than me."

Reece shook his head, picked up his burger, ate, then after leaving money on the counter, he left. This was ridiculous.

Chapter Seven

Saturday, just two days later, Reece entered the diner again, waved, or nodded to those who called out to him, and took a seat at the counter then looked around. The place was packed as usual. He wondered if Rissa was working and got his answer when he saw her enter from the kitchen area. He knew the minute she saw him too because she hesitated in her steps. She moved to the coffee machine and picked up a carafe and made her way toward him but stopped along the way to refill cups. When she finally stood in front of him, she placed a cup down and raised an eyebrow at him in question. He nodded, and she poured him a cup of coffee.

"Do you want to order?"

"In a minute. I'm waiting for my brother." He could see dark circles under her eyes, and he knew he was the cause of them. Damn, he wanted to kick his own ass.

"Fine," she said then spun on her heel and headed back to the kitchen.

She was still pissed at him. He ran his hand around the back of his neck, knowing he had to grow some balls and talk to her. He was about to get up when the bell over the door rang, and he glanced over to see Cord enter. His brother nodded then took a seat beside him. Rissa came from the kitchen again, picked up the carafe, then walked to where he and Cord sat.

"Coffee?" she asked Cord.

"Yes, ma'am, please."

Rissa poured him coffee then set the carafe behind her on the counter and pulled out her pad and pencil.

"Ready to order, or do you need more time?"

Reece saw Cord glance between him and Rissa with a frown on his face.

"I, uh, don't need more time. Do you Reece?"

"No. I'll take my usual."

"And what would that be?" she asked him then blew a bubble with her gum and popped it.

He clenched his jaw. She knew damn well what his usual was. Talk about being hardheaded. This woman was still driving him insane.

"Cheeseburger with everything and onion rings, as if you didn't know," he growled out, making Cord narrow his eyes at him.

"A lot of people come in. How am I supposed to remember everyone's usual?" She wrote it on her pad then looked at Cord.

"This is my brother, Cord. Cord, Rissa Gates."

"Nice to meet you," she said and smiled at him.

"I'll have the same, thank you."

"*You're* welcome," she said then walked to the wheel, attached the orders, turned the wheel around then disappeared into the kitchen.

"What's with the attitude? You want to tell me what that was about?" Cord asked him.

"No," he snapped. When Cord chuckled, he glared at him, making Cord laugh harder. "That damn woman is going to be the death of me."

"Hell, but what a way to go. She's gorgeous."

He turned on the stool to face his brother. "Back the fuck off, *little* brother." He twisted to face the counter and picked up his cup to take a sip of the hot brew.

"Hmm…sounds like she might be a bit under your skin. And what do you mean by little? We're the same height, weight, and build, although I'd say I'm *bigger* than you in some areas."

Reece choked on his coffee and sputtered out a laugh. Cord could always make him laugh when he was angry about something. He looked at Cord to see him grinning at him like he knew something he didn't. Reece shook his head then both men sat in silence as they waited for their food.

****

Rissa hopped up on the stool and tried to calm her breathing. Damn him for coming in here. Couldn't he and his brother eat somewhere else? There was a great restaurant in Hartland. She jumped down and peeked out the server window to look at Reece. His brother was hot too. He had the same eyes as Reece. Both men were swoon-worthy but damn Reece Maddox had her heart, and he didn't even want it.

She sniffled then took a seat back on the stool to wait for their lunches to be finished. She mentally groaned when she thought about carrying them back out there and seeing Reece again. She loved him so much, but she'd be

162

damned before she'd be all nice and sweet with him. He broke her heart, and she wanted nothing more to do with him. No matter how hot it had been between them, she was done being a fool. She should have known not to get involved but like Deidra told her, she had to take a chance or she'd regret it. She couldn't imagine having not, at least, giving it a try. She just ached inside, knowing she'd never have him in her life again.

A few minutes later, her uncle told her the orders were up. After huffing out a breath, she jumped down from the stool, placed the food on a tray, and walked to where *he* sat. She set the plates down on the counter.

"Can I get you anything else?"

"No, ma'am," Cord said.

"I'm good, thank you," Reece said as he looked at her.

She nodded then entered the kitchen. She couldn't look at him. He was the love of her life, but she'd never be the love of his. She choked back a sob as she sat on the stool. Glancing at the clock, she was happy to see her shift was over. She planned to go to Dewey's tonight just to get out and have a good time. She deserved that.

Pulling her apron off, she hung it up, and took her coat down, tugged it on then her beanie. After telling her aunt goodbye, she headed outside with her uncle beside her. She climbed the steps to her apartment then looked down at her uncle at the bottom of the stairs, waved then entered the apartment. She was going to have a long soak in her tub then get ready to paint the town. Too bad a certain gorgeous cowboy wasn't painting it with her. After locking the door, she removed her coat, and hat then hung them up and headed for the bathroom. She just hoped Nolan wasn't around to see her walking to Dewey's alone. Her family would have a fit if they knew.

Three hours later, Rissa sat on a stool at the bar in Dewey's and scanned the crowd. The place was packed. She had never been here before but had heard it was a real cowboy bar, and she could see that was true by all the hats. On the dance floor, in the pool room, and at pinball machines. Also, the bar was lined with them and the tables were full.

"Would you like another drink, Rissa?"

She glanced over to see Laura Carson, one of the barmaids at Dewey's. Rissa smiled. She had met Laura on New Year's Eve at a party in Spring City.

"Yes, please. Callahan Whiskey on the rocks."

"You got it. I'll be right back."

She watched Laura move to the glass shelves opposite the bar, get the bottle down, pour it over ice in a glass, and head back to her. She set the glass down on a napkin.

"Enjoy, Rissa. Just flag me down if you need anything else."

"I will, Laura, thank you." Rissa picked up the glass and took a sip. It brought back memories of the night with Reece in Helena. "Damn that man," she muttered.

"Hey, babe, you wanna dance?" a cowboy slurred beside her.

"No, thank you. I just want to enjoy my drink for now."

"Maybe later then." He tipped his hat then weaved through the tables.

She chuckled. He'd probably never remember he had asked. She watched Laura buzz around behind the bar. The woman didn't seem to stop. She refilled glasses, put beer in front of people, and still found time to place baskets of pretzels and peanuts on the bar. She was a beautiful woman with blonde hair and thick, lush lashes that surrounded her golden hazel eyes. Most of the men who came in here tried to talk to her, but she was too busy unless her husband Jeb came in. Rissa knew how Laura felt about Jeb. Just about everyone did, and Jeb knew he didn't have to worry about Laura straying. They'd been married for years and acted like they were still dating. Laura loved her man, and she'd told Rissa she hadn't been able to resist Jeb when they first started dating. She knew how Laura felt. If Reece showed up right now and wanted her to go home with him, she'd go with him in a heartbeat.

Speak of the devil. Rissa watched as Jeb took a seat at the bar and kept his eyes on Laura, then she turned and spotted him. Rissa saw Jeb grin at Laura, and she strolled to him, leaned over the bar, and kissed him, making Rissa sigh. Damn, Jeb was a good-looking man too. He was about six foot, and solidly built. He wore his blond hair short. A black cowboy hat covered his head, and his lower face, jaw, and neck were covered in stubble. Biting her lip, she used to love to scrape her fingernails across Reece's scruff. She thought it was so sexy. Even when he had been cleanshaven, she could see a faint shadow. It looked like Jeb was the same.

Just like Reece, Jeb's sideburns ended at the lobe of his ear and blended into the shadow. What the hell was it about the men in this area? So many gorgeous ones here, in Spring City, and Hartland, and so many of them with dark brown or black hair. A real weakness for her even though Nolan was blond. That right there should have told her something. He wasn't really her type. She finished the drink and signaled Laura she wanted a refill.

"You here alone?"

"Yes, but I walked so don't worry."

"All right, but if you need a ride, I can get Jeb to drive you home."

She leaned over the bar. "You'd trust another woman with that fine man of yours?"

Laura laughed. "I trust *him*. Not sure about the other women."

Rissa raised her glass. "I sure wouldn't. He's gorgeous, Laura."

"He is, and I love that he's mine."

"Unlike me with Reece. Damn him, anyway."

"Reece might change his mind. Jeb was the same. He never wanted to get married." Laura shrugged.

"I know Reece's excuse but that doesn't make it any easier."

"I know. I'm sorry, Rissa. Hang in there."

"I'm trying. And men say we're hard to understand."

"*Pffft*, I'm an open book compared to Jeb now." Laura laughed.

"We women are quite easy to understand. Men just don't want to see that." She shook her head. *Damn Reece Maddox.*

Six drinks later, Rissa was on the dance floor in a line dance. She was laughing and having a ball. She knew Laura was keeping an eye on her though. She just wanted to forget Reece Maddox for a while. Maybe when she got back home, she'd fall into bed and sleep until morning. She wasn't scheduled to work until Monday and since it was Saturday, she was free the rest of the weekend. Spinning around in the line, she paused to wait for the dizziness to pass. The six drinks must be catching up to her. Making her way off the floor, she walked to the bathroom, entered, and looked in the mirror. *You don't look drunk.* But suddenly she started to giggle.

The door opened and two women entered and smiled at her. She turned on the water and splashed cold water on her wrists. She didn't know if that worked but it felt good. After one last look at herself, she took a deep breath and headed back to the bar. She hopped up on the stool and waved at Laura.

"Rissa, I think you've had enough," Laura said shaking her head.

"Oh, come on, just one more," she pleaded, frowning at how she'd slurred her words.

"I have the right to refuse anyone and you, my friend, are being refused."

"Fine, I'll go home then."

"Sit here a few minutes. Take a breather then you can go. Are you sure you don't want Jeb to drive you home?"

"Positive. The cold air will do me good. I'm fine." She waved her hand around. She turned the stool to watch the people on the dance floor and bounced her foot on the footrest while listening to the band play *Pontoon*, a Little Big Town song.

"Hey, sweetheart," a male voice said from beside her. She looked over to see a young, good-looking cowboy.

"Hey, yourself," she said with a smile.

"Can I buy you a drink?"

"Just a root beer is fine. I've had too many," she said then giggled.

He grinned at her. "All right." He signaled to one of the bartenders.

"What can I get ya?" the bartender asked him.

"The lady will have a root beer, and I'll have a beer, whatever you have on tap."

The bartender tapped the bar. "I'll be right back."

Rissa glanced around and saw Jeb on his cellphone but looking at her. She frowned at him, but he turned away.

"What's your name, sweetheart?"

"Darissa Gates, but everyone calls me Rish-Rish-*Rissa*. What's yours?"

"Landon Jewell. Nice to meet you, Miss Rissa," he said with a smile.

She smiled. The bartender set her root beer and Landon's beer down. Landon pulled his wallet from his back pocket, paid the bartender, and waved away the change. The bartender thanked him then walked off. She picked up her glass and took a sip. It was good, but it was no Callahan Whiskey. She'd really love another one, but she knew she was feeling more than a little tipsy. Hell though, she was walking home. She leaned toward Landon.

"How about we grab a table, and you get me a Callahan Whiskey on the rocks. Laura cut me off." She laughed.

"Laura?" he asked with a frown.

"The barmaid."

"I don't know. If she thinks you've had enough—"

"Whatever." Rissa huffed.

"Hey, don't get mad, hon. I just don't want you driving."

"I'm walking. I live above the diner and it's just a few blocks up the street."

"I really don't know where that is. I'm just passing through. A bunch of us are heading to Kalispell for a rodeo."

"Do you compete?"

"I'm a bullfighter."

"Wow, you guys are crazy."

Landon chuckled. "Yeah, we are."

They talked for a while then she knew she needed to leave. She jumped down from the barstool. "I need to go."

"Oh, hey, don't go yet...at least let me walk you home."

She didn't know this guy at all, but hell, she hadn't known Reece the night she met him either.

"All—"

"I'll be walking her home. You get lost."

Rissa looked up to see Reece standing beside her but leaning an elbow on the bar. She gasped then looked at Landon.

"*He* is *not* walking me home. *You* can."

Landan looked Reece up and down then stepped closer to him.

"She said I'm walking her home."

"Back the fuck off, kid, or I will knock you into next week." Reece straightened up to his full height, making Landon step back. He tipped his hat at Rissa, turned, and disappeared into the crowd.

"What did you do that for?"

"You don't know him, and you're drunk," Reece growled out.

"I didn't know you either," she snapped.

"Yeah and look how that turned out. Besides, you weren't drunk that night. You want to take that guy home and fuck him? Then, by all means, go for it." He stared at her with narrowed eyes.

"I will walk myself home." She took her coat off the back of the stool, pulled it on then moved through the crowd, but stopped alongside Jeb. "Thanks a lot."

"What the hell did I do?" Jeb asked trying to look innocent.

"You called Reece!"

Jeb looked embarrassed. "I didn't want you making a mistake, Rissa."

"I already made one." She pointed at Reece then pushed through the crowd, shoved the door open, and stepped out into the cold. She began marching up the street toward her apartment. When she heard footsteps behind her, Rissa turned around to see Reece following her. "Go away."

****

Reece watched as she continued but when Rissa stumbled, he grabbed her arms to catch her from falling.

"I'm walking home. Leave me alone, Reece," she slurred her words.

"You're in no condition to walk that far," he growled out.

"Nonetheless, I *am* walking, so get your hands off me. You don't have time to fool with me...remember?"

He removed his hands from her arms and watched as she turned away from him then made her way across the street. He had heard the pain in her voice.

"Son of a bitch," he muttered then took a deep breath and followed her.

There was no way he could let her walk to her apartment in the condition she was in. He caught up to her just as she made her way to the sidewalk. Walking behind her, he tried not to look at her ass in those tight jeans, but his eyes seemed to have a mind of their own. She was wearing a short jacket and her ass was making him want to grab it and squeeze it in his hands. He came to a sudden halt when she spun around and glared at him.

"What do you think you're doing, Maddox?"

"Just taking a walk." It took every ounce of his willpower not to grab her, pull her close, and kiss those soft lips.

"*Pffft*. You're not taking a walk, you're following me. I'm fine. Actually, I'm doing pretty good for the shape I'm in." She placed her hands on her hips and narrowed her eyes at him even as she wobbled a bit.

"I just happen to be going the same way as you." He shrugged.

"You're so full of it. Whatever." She waved her hand around, then turned and started walking away from him.

"You want to tell me why you're out here anyway? Did you walk to the bar too?" he asked.

"Yes."

"Damn it, Rissa. You know you're not supposed to be out here alone. McCabe could be out here just waiting for you," he growled.

She stopped then turned around to look at him.

"I am tired of being...*escorted* every damn place I go. Including now! Leave me alone, Maddox." She raised her middle finger at him then turned and walked away from him.

He stayed a few feet behind her and watched her weave her way up the sidewalk as if she were moving around objects but when they finally reached the diner, he jogged up to her when she stopped, bent at the waist, and braced her hands on her knees.

"Are you all right?"

"I don't feel so good," she murmured.

"Quit being so fucking hardheaded and let me help you. You're a little intoxicated."

"I am not intox...a...micated," she slurred.

"*Intoximicated?* Sure, you're not that. Let's go."

Rissa slowly straightened up and turned to look at him. She nodded her head then threw up in his direction. He tried to jump back, but she got the toes of his good boots, then he narrowed his eyes at her and clenched his jaw when she threw her hand over her mouth, but laughter bubbled out.

"Oops," she said with a laugh.

"*Oops?* That's all you can say? You just threw up on a four-hundred-dollar pair of boots."

"I didn't do it on purpose." She laughed more.

"You think that's funny?"

She cleared her throat and looked up at him then shook her head.

"No. I'm really sorry. I guess I...drank too mush."

"Too *mush?* Ya think?" He shook his head then walked to the building, where he kicked the toe of his boots against it to try to remove whatever it was on them. He didn't even want to think about it then he walked back to her. "Come on. I'll walk you up."

She leaned close to him. "I'm sho shorry."

"Please don't breathe on me." He waved his hand in front of her face. "To say your breath is bad would be a huge understatement."

"I threw up. What do you expect?"

"I expect you to not talk in my face and to please brush your teeth."

"You never complained before."

"Because you didn't have the stench of vomit coming from your mouth."

She burst out laughing. "True."

She turned from him, started walking, and almost fell. He caught her around the waist, helped her around the back of the diner, and up the steps.

"I really thought you could hold your liquor better than this. How many did you have?"

"I had shix whishkeys."

"Christ! Six? No wonder you can't walk."

"I can walk."

"Stumbling is not walking." Reece held onto her as they climbed the stairs. He watched as she fumbled to get her key in the lock, so he took it from her, inserted it, opened the door, and led her to the sofa where she flopped down. She looked up at him with those sexy green eyes and he wanted to beg her to come home with him.

"Thank you."

"Yes, ma'am." He cleared his throat. "I need a paper towel to try to clean my boots off," he muttered as he entered the kitchen. He tore a towel off the rack, ran it under water then cleaned his boots. After tossing it into the trash and washing his hands, he headed back into the living room to see her still on the sofa. "Rissa? Come home with me."

"I have bad breath."

"True. You could kill an elephant with that breath."

She fell to the side, her face landing on the cushion, and laughed.

He huffed out a breath. "Okay, never mind. I'll call you tomorrow to see how you are but I'm sure you'll have one hell of a hangover. If you change your mind, you know where to find me, but brush your teeth first." He grinned when she giggled.

Striding to the door, he opened it, turned the lock, stepped out, and closed it behind him. He trotted down the steps and headed back to Dewey's, where he left his truck. It was a cold night but soon warmer weather would arrive, and he was so ready for it. He needed to get back to work and being out in the field was a lot easier when the weather was nice. He strode down the sidewalk then crossed the street when he was near the bar. The music could be heard from inside, and louder when the door opened, but he stopped when he thought he heard someone behind him. He shook his head then headed for the parking lot.

As he reached Dewey's, he headed around to the back since he hadn't been able to find a spot out front when he arrived. He put his hand into his coat pocket, pulled out his keys, aimed the fob at his truck to see the lights flash. He turned when someone yelled his last name and took a hit to the side of his face, knocking him back. He gained his footing and looked over to see McCabe standing there with a nasty grin on his face.

"Is that the only way you can take someone down? By a surprise attack?" Reece narrowed his eyes at the man.

"I got your attention, didn't I? Let's do this, cowboy."

Reece strode toward him and got kicked in the ribs, making him fall to his knees. He glared at McCabe.

"I thought it would be a little harder than this to kick your ass," McCabe said.

Reece got to his feet and scowled at him.

"You're going to have to try a lot harder, you little prick," he said through clenched teeth.

McCabe laughed and moved closer toward him, then stopped, and put his hand up and motioned for Reece to come at him. Taking a deep breath, he stepped forward but stopped. His damn ribs were killing him, and this little bastard better not have cracked them. It sure felt like it though.

"Come on, Maddox. You afraid of me?"

"In your dreams. I'm not afraid of a man who intimidates a woman. You want to do this. You come to me." He widened his stance but kept his hands at his sides.

McCabe grinned and moved closer. Reece swung at him, but Nolan ducked and kicked out, hitting him in the gut. With a grunt, Reece dropped to his knees again.

"You may not be afraid of me, but I can still kick your ass."

"How about you quit dancing around and fight me like a man?"

McCabe stopped bouncing. "It's called karate, not dancing. I have a black belt. It's how men fight."

"Not this man. Put your fists up and fight, you fucking pussy." He got to his feet again.

When McCabe stepped forward, he clenched his fists. All he needed was one good shot. McCabe stopped within five feet of him, smirked, and held his arms out.

"Here I am, cowboy. Come and get me."

"What the hell did she ever see in you?"

"You just want to fuck her," McCabe said through clenched teeth.

"And you just want to scare her into making her stay with you." Reece smirked. "Did you know when she left you in August, she spent the night with me in Helena?" He knew by the look on McCabe's face that what he said surprised him. Reece made a move, but McCabe spun around and kicked him in the side of the head. Reece stumbled back against his truck, fell to the ground, and lost consciousness.

Blinking against the brightness of the room, Reece looked to his side to see Rissa sitting in a chair beside the bed.

"What happened?" he asked.

"No one is really sure. A couple of guys found you beside your truck in Dewey's parking lot."

"Son of a bitch," he muttered, then tried to sit up and hissed in a breath. "He cracked one of my ribs, didn't he?"

"Who?"

He narrowed his eyes as he glared at her.

"You know damn well who. I will kick that little prick's ass."

"Not for a while you won't, Mr. Maddox," a doctor said as she entered the room. "You don't have a cracked rib, but it is severely bruised, and you have a mild concussion. You won't be kicking anyone's ass for some time."

"I'm going home," Reece said, as he sat up, gasped in pain, then collapsed back against the pillow as throbbing pain ripped through his side and head.

"You can't yet, Reece," Rissa said.

"Why the hell are you even here?" When she drew in a deep breath, he felt like an ass. "Sorry," he muttered then watched as she stood.

"I'll be going then." She picked up her coat from another chair then strode from the room without looking back.

"Damn it," he said and wondered why he acted like this when he'd just asked her to go home with him.

"I know you're in pain, but no need to take it out on someone else. I'd like to keep you overnight for observation," the doctor said.

"No. I'm going home. I'll call someone to come and get me, but I'm not staying here." He frowned. "How long have I been here anyway?"

"You were brought in last night and you were in and out quite a bit. I can't make you stay but if you do leave, make sure you have someone check on you."

"I'll have my ranch manager's wife do it."

"All right. See that you do. I'll be right back with your discharge papers. Make sure you follow the instructions. No doing anything to make your brain work too hard. That means no computer or TV for a while. Ice on those ribs might help. Try not to cough, sneeze, or breathe deeply. Got it?"

"Yes, ma'am." Reece leaned his head back on the pillow. The doctor left the room. Once again, he had hurt Rissa. "You'd think she'd learn to stay the hell away from you," he murmured.

****

Rissa sat in her vehicle with tears rolling down her face.

"Damn you, Reece Maddox. You're the biggest prick I know." She shook her head. "Next biggest, after Nolan."

She had almost passed out when Deidra told her Reece was in the hospital. Her sister and Preston had shown up at her door early this morning to let her know. Preston looked mad enough to kill someone. She followed them to the hospital, and when they entered the room Reece was in, it took all her strength to look at him lying there with bruises all over his face. Preston told her that Sam had called Cord, and Cord then called him.

178

Cord was sitting in the chair beside the bed and she could see he was worried about his brother. He left not long after she arrived. No one had seen anything, no witnesses, but she knew who had done this. It didn't take a genius to realize it was Nolan. Now Reece was hurt because of her.

"Why do you keep tormenting yourself with this man? He doesn't want you," she whispered as fresh tears fell. She started the car then drove out of the parking lot to head home.

A few hours later, she sat in the kitchen of the diner and watched her uncle make dinner for customers. A salad sat in front of her, but she had no appetite and not because of the hangover she was trying to ignore. She wondered how Reece was doing, but she'd be damned before she'd call him.

"You need to eat," Connie said as she passed by.

"I'm really not hungry, Aunt Connie." She pushed the lettuce around with her fork.

"Hey," Deidra said as she entered the kitchen, took off her coat and hat then hung them up. She lifted an apron off the peg and pulled it over her head.

"I didn't think you were coming in," Connie said.

"I wasn't, but Preston is getting the cattle in, and I don't have any illustrations to do right now so..." She shrugged. "I was bored."

"Well, you won't be bored here. I suppose since the weather warmed up a little, everyone is out and about." Connie picked up a tray and carried it out to the dining area.

"Are you all right?" Deidra asked Rissa.

"I'm fine. I just need to keep telling myself to stay away from Reece. He doesn't want me." She hiccupped on a sob.

Deidra put her arm around her. "I wish I knew what to tell you. Preston picked him up at the hospital and took him home. He said he tried to help Reece inside his house, but he just about tore his head off, so he watched him make his way inside then went home."

"I know it was Nolan who did this to him. I wish I had never come here. If I hadn't then Reece wouldn't be hurt, and Nolan wouldn't be here causing problems."

"No, he wouldn't be here, but he'd still be causing problems with you, Rissa. He's a jerk. He needs to leave here and leave you alone."

"I don't see that happening." Rissa jumped down from the stool, threw what was left of her salad into the trash then pulled on an apron. "I know I'm off today, but I need something to do. I'm going out to take orders."

****

Two days later, Reece sat in the recliner watching TV when there was a knock on his door. Skipper jumped up and ran for the kitchen.

"Come in," he yelled, then immediately regretted it. His ribs and head still hurt.

"It's me, Sam."

"In the living room, Sam."

Sam entered with Skipper behind him and took a seat on the sofa and stared at Reece while rubbing the dog's ears.

"You look like shit."

"Well hell, Sam. Say what you think."

Sam grinned. "Sorry. How are you feeling?"

"Been better, but I'm getting there."

"Want to tell me what happened?" Sam leaned back and placed his booted foot on his knee.

Reece shrugged. "Can't remember."

"Bullshit. I know who did this to you, and you know I do, so just tell me."

"Nope. I'll take care of it."

"Not a good idea. He might be a little shit but knowing karate like he does, you might not get the chance to take care of it."

"He wouldn't fight me like a man. I'll get him."

"I did not hear this. I know if I say not to do anything, you're going to ignore me, but damn it, Reece, I can't let you go after him without telling you not to."

"Understood. You told me not to go after him. I got it."

"Damn hardhead. Don't make me have to arrest you. Do not go too far."

"Payback's a bitch, Sam. That jackass is going down. Don't worry, I won't kill him, but I plan to repay the favor."

Sam blew out a breath, stood, and gazed down at him.

"Do you need anything?"

"No, I'm good. Terry's wife has been coming in to check on me."

"I thought Rissa would do that."

Reece cleared his throat. "I doubt I'll see much of her after the way I ran her off at the hospital."

"I don't know why you act the way you do with her. Rissa is a wonderful woman."

"I can't give her what she wants," Reece muttered.

"Yeah, that's bullshit too. You could if you'd man up. I'll see you later. Remember what I said, don't make me run your ass in." Sam touched the brim of his hat and strode from the living room.

Reece heard the kitchen door open and close.

Blowing out a breath, he knew Sam didn't understand about him and Rissa. Hell, he didn't understand it himself. That was a lie. He knew precisely why he couldn't give her what she wanted. Between his mother, father, and Cord, their relationship failures had made him a cynic when it came to love. Sure, his friends were happy...for now. He just didn't believe love could really last. He'd seen too many relationships fall apart to believe in it.

But Preston and Deidra seemed happy, and Preston hadn't been this happy, ever. Reece thought Preston had been happy with Glenda, but he always seemed so tense. Like he had the weight of the world on his shoulders. He wasn't like that with Deidra. He was genuinely happy.

And Sam, hell, he was so in love with his wife, Tessa. But then again, he was just like Reece's other friends. All of them were very much in love and over the top happy. Some had families now, and others were working on that.

"And here you sit...alone," he muttered.

In all honesty, he wasn't sure he wanted to risk putting his heart on the line. He'd avoided love for the longest time. Oh sure, he loved his friends, horses, and a dog, but never had he loved a woman.

Liar. This feeling for Rissa was so deep in his heart that the thought of not having her in his life scared him more than having her in it. But he'd pushed her away once again. Hell. Pushing back on the chair, he reclined it as far back as it could go, closed his eyes, and wondered if she'd ever speak to him again.

What the fuck is wrong with you? Just the other night, you were asking her to come home with you. Idiot!

About an hour later, someone knocked on his door. He heard it open then Preston entered the room. *Hell, this can't be good.* He watched as his friend removed his coat and hat, placed them over the back of the sofa then took a seat, and stared at him.

"Say whatever the hell you're here to say, then you can go."

Preston smirked. "You know me too well." He took a deep breath. "Okay, what the fuck is wrong with you?"

"Christ, Preston, you know how I feel about things. You know what I grew up with."

"I know you're full of shit. I know you got on me all the time about how bad I had it for Deidra, and yet here you are feeling the same way about Rissa."

"Bullshit," he snapped then clenched his teeth when Preston laughed.

"Deny it all you want, my friend, but you have got it bad and I don't get it—"

"You do get it! You know my parents. You know how many times they've been married. I think they're competing. Which one can marry the most people in their lifetime? Cord told me Dad is getting yet another divorce."

"Yeah, I know all about them, but you're not them, Reece."

"My family has no luck in love. Look at Cord."

"Cord loves Faith and he always will. Even though they're not together, you have to see that his love for her has never faded."

"I know he'll always love her, but she broke his heart."

"Yes, she did, but I bet if she wanted him back, he'd take her back." Preston shrugged. "He loves her. Always will so don't give me shit about love not lasting. Most of your friends are married and in love with their wives. I love Deidra and I know I will until I take my last breath. You could have that."

"And what if Rissa doesn't want that even though she thinks she does. I won't take the chance that Rissa would leave me. I won't."

"You shouldn't go into a marriage looking at a divorce, Reece." Preston pushed to his feet and stared down at him. "You're scared, I get that but hell, so was I. After the number Glenda did on me, I swore I'd never fall again then a petite brunette entered my life and I can't imagine ever being without her."

"Exactly, Preston. I don't want to imagine how it would be."

"You don't have to imagine it, Reece. You're living it." Preston picked up his hat, put it on then shrugged on his coat, and walked out of the living room. Reece heard the kitchen door open and close behind him.

Blowing out a breath, he wasn't sure what to think. He was damned if he did and damned if he didn't. Not all relationships last but how many does a man need to go through before he finds one that will.

A little while later, he heard a knock on his door again. It was like damn Grand Central Station here today. He was about to get up when he heard the door open and close then his father appeared in the doorway. Reece mentally groaned.

"Dad? What are you doing here?"

"I heard you were hurt. I didn't get by to see you when you were shot since I was out of town, but I just got word from your brother that you were hurt again." His father removed his coat, hat, gloves, placed them on the arm of the sofa then took a seat.

"I'm fine."

"You don't look fine, son. What happened?"

"Just someone took me by surprise. Over a damn woman."

"You? Fighting over a woman?"

"Not in that way. He's an old boyfriend of someone I was seeing." Reece shrugged.

"*Was* seeing?"

"Let it go, Dad. It's over anyway." Reece glanced at him. "I hear you're getting another divorce?"

His father winced. "Yes. It seems I can't find the right one."

"Bullshit. What you can't do is keep it in your pants. Why the fuck do you bother getting married? Just fuck around," Reece snapped.

"Do not talk to me in that manner, Reece," his father said in a stern voice.

Reece immediately regretted it. "I'm sorry. I just don't understand why you and Mom are never happy."

"We were. My job took me away all the time. Hell, you know how it is. Being a Livestock agent, you're on the go most of the time. Especially in the theft department."

"So, that's your excuse? Your job? How many women did you fool around with while on your job? Look, Dad, I'm sorry but I don't believe that. You made your decisions and probably lost the one good woman you had. Mom."

His father sighed. "You're probably right but there's nothing I can do about that now. She's finally happy."

"Well, at least one of us in this family is."

"I know I've sullied you on love, Reece, but don't go by me. Shit happens all the time. Not all love lasts but a lot of it does. Let me tell you this—I will always love your mother but I'm the one who screwed it up, not her. If I could go back—"

"Yeah, well you can't. None of us can. You'll get married again because you can't help yourself. I won't go down that path because I don't want to be like you. I love you, Dad, but you're the worst role model there is for lasting love." He leaned his head back and closed his eyes.

"I'm sorry you feel that way. Maybe one day you'll find the love of your life and when you do, I hope you don't let her go. No matter what. Not unless she wants to go but I believe if you do your part, she won't."

He opened his eyes to see his father putting on his coat, hat, and gloves then he was gone.

"If I do my part? Shit, I've already fucked that up," Reece mumbled as he closed his eyes again.

Chapter Eight

Rissa sat in her apartment and stared at the TV but didn't see anything. She wanted to punch Nolan for hurting Reece. The man just healed from being shot, and now Nolan had put him in the hospital from a beating. Damn it. This was all her fault. If she hadn't come here, maybe she would have been able to convince Nolan it was over. She knew his way of thinking. If he was close, she belonged to him.

She wondered how Reece was doing. Why had she even gone to the hospital? A sudden thought took hold in her mind and she quickly sat up.

"He asked me to go home with him the other night," she exclaimed.

Then why did he run her off from the hospital? She reached for her phone and called her sister.

"Hey, Rissa, what's up?" Deidra answered.

"Has Preston checked on Reece?"

"Yeah, he just got back from seeing him. Why?"

"I'm going out there."

"Rissa, I don't think that's a good idea. I know I told you to go for it, but I think it's best if you just get over him."

"Could you get over Preston?" Rissa snapped.

"Well, no..."

"Then you know how I feel. I-I...love him, Deidra. I'm going to be with him as much as I can even if he doesn't want anything more from me. I'll talk to you tomorrow. I'm going to see if Lanie can cover for me tomorrow."

"I will. I finished my drawings for the other book. I'll take your shift."

"Thank you. I'll call you. Love you." Rissa hit *End*, stood, walked to her bedroom to change clothes then headed down the stairs, not even thinking of Nolan being around, got into her SUV, and headed for Reece's place. The damn man was going to be the death of her. She would not leave, no matter what he said this time.

Pulling into his driveway, she drove up to the back porch, parked, then climbed the steps to the porch. She smiled when she heard Skipper barking. Taking a deep breath, she blew it out and knocked on the door. She heard Reece telling Skipper to be quiet then the door opened, and she wanted to cry at the bruises on his face.

"Rissa? What are you doing here?"

"You asked me to come home with you Saturday night." She folded her arms and tapped her foot as she looked up at him. Even with a huge bruise on his cheek, he was still the most handsome man she'd ever seen.

"A moment of weakness," he retorted.

She pushed past him and entered the kitchen then removed her coat and hung it up on the pegs.

"I think the weather is finally breaking. I can't wait to see this town in the spring and summer."

"Why are you here?" Reece repeated.

"I came here to help you—"

"I don't need any help. I can get around just fine. My ribs are bruised but ice is helping, so no need for you to be here."

She slowly moved to him and bit back a grin when he straightened up and narrowed his eyes at her. She put her arms around his waist, stood on her toes, and kissed his bruised cheek. She heard him draw in a breath.

"Did I hurt you?" she whispered.

"No. No, you didn't hurt me," he whispered back.

"Any other place you need kissed?"

His arms wrapped around her. "Oh, sweetheart, you have no idea."

She laughed then looked up at him. "I think I do. I'm so sorry he did this to you."

"I'm not done. I'll get him."

"Reece, he could have hurt you a lot worse."

"All I need is one good punch and it *will* happen."

"Please don't."

"Are you afraid I'll hurt him? Is that it?"

"No! I don't want him hurting you any more than he already has."

"I can handle him. He caught me off guard but it won't happen again." He took a deep breath. "Well, since you're here, come into the living room and sit with me."

She smiled up at him. "Okay."

Reece took her hand in his and led her to the living room then he lowered himself slowly onto the sofa and she sat down beside him. When he winced in pain, she blinked back tears.

"Reece, do you have pain meds you can take? I can get them for you."

"I do but I hate taking them. They kick my ass."

"Rest is probably best for you. Where are they? I'll get them."

"Are you going to take advantage of me while I'm stoned on those pills?" he asked her with a grin.

"Damn right, I will." She pushed up from the sofa. "Where are they?"

"Medicine cabinet in my bathroom."

Much later, Rissa jerked awake and glanced around the dark room. It came to her that she was in Reece's bed. Reaching over to touch him, she found the bed empty. Lying beside him was torture because they couldn't have sex. He was in a lot of pain yet. She looked at the clock to see it was close to two in the morning. Throwing the covers back, she swung her legs over the side, stood then walked around to the other side of the bed, and picked up his T-shirt. After pulling it over her head, and down her body, she noticed the lights were on in the pool. Walking to the glass door, she peered out and saw him. He was swimming, doing laps. He looked like an Olympic swimmer the way he'd turn and put his feet against the wall, push off, then swim underwater for almost the entire length of the pool. The underwater lights allowed her to see him, and she could see he was nude. He had told her he used the pool at night if he couldn't sleep.

Sliding the door open, she stepped onto the deck and watched him. It was freezing out, but she couldn't tear her eyes from him. He moved through the water without even making waves. She wondered if his ribs were bothering him but with the way he was swimming, it didn't look like it. He surfaced at the opposite end, shook his head to dispel water then turned in her direction. He grinned at her, pushed off the wall, and swam underwater to the end where she stood. He came up, placed his arms on the cement surrounding the pool, and stared up at her.

"Aren't you cold?"

"Yes, but I like watching you swim." Her teeth began to chatter.

"Then come on in," he said with a grin.

She tugged his shirt off over her head, dropped it on the deck then jumped into the pool. When she surfaced, Reece was beside her. His arms wrapped around her and pulled her close to him.

"You are so beautiful," he murmured against her lips before taking them in a deep kiss.

"Don't hurt yourself," she said when he released her mouth.

"I'll be fine. I need you, Rissa. I've missed you."

"Reece, in the hospital...what you said...you hurt me."

"I know. I'm sorry. It was just that when you asked me who, when you knew as well as I did who did this to me, it pissed me off. I lashed out." He kissed her forehead. "It was wrong of me to take it out on you."

"I get that, but please make up your mind about us seeing each other."

"I can't promise you anything, Rissa. What we do is up to you."

Blinking back tears, it really hit her that she was wasting her time with this man, but she couldn't seem to stay away. She loved him and she'd take what she could get with him. She was a fool where he was concerned. He was never going to settle down with her, or anyone for that matter.

She shook her head. "I know I'm going to end up with a broken heart but I—"

"Don't fall in love with me, Rissa."

"Too late," she whispered.

"Damn it—"

"Please, just let it go for now. It's all on me. It's my heart."

He blew out a breath. "I don't want you hurt."

"Well, I'm going to be no matter how you look at it—whether I stay or go."

Reece shook his head and moved away from her. She watched him swim toward the steps, climbed them, and walked to the deck. He picked up a towel, dried off then entered the house.

****

Reece swore as he entered the bathroom. Reaching into the stall, he turned the shower on and stepped inside. He picked up the shampoo, squirted some into his hand, and scrubbed the chlorine from his hair. *Son of a bitch.* He should have just cut it off with her a long time ago, but he couldn't stay away from her.

Now she says she loves him. He rubbed a spot over his heart. Knowing that didn't make him panic like it usually did. *What the hell did that mean?*

He jerked when the door opened, and Rissa stepped inside. She didn't say a word, just picked up the shampoo and washed her hair. He could see the tears in her eyes and if it were at all possible, he'd give himself a swift kick in the ass for hurting her. Once she rinsed her hair, she opened the door, grabbed a towel, and stepped out. Leaving him there and wondering what the hell he was going to do about this.

After taking a deep breath, he scrubbed his body clean, opened the door, took a towel off the rack, dried off, stepped out then wrapped the towel around his waist. He grabbed another one to rub his wet hair, then entered the bedroom to see her sitting on the edge of the bed.

"Rissa?"

"You don't have to say anything, Reece. I knew this could happen going in."

"Look, Rissa, I've seen my dad go through five wives, and he's getting divorced again. My mother is on her third husband. Love fades. It doesn't last," he said with a shrug and watched her clench her jaw then she glared up at him.

"You are so full of shit. Your dad can't find what he wants. That has nothing to do with love. If he loved any of them, he'd stay, but he doesn't. He's never happy, and it sounds like your mother isn't either."

"And my brother? So, he's not happy either? Yeah, you'd be right about that because the woman he loves chose a career over him," he snapped.

"People fall in love and get their hearts broken every day. It's a chance we all take." She got to her feet, found her clothes, and began to dress.

"Well, I'm not willing to take that chance." He frowned as he watched her put her clothes on. "Where are you going?"

She whirled around to glare at him. "Away from you before I throat punch you. There is no sense in me sticking around any longer, Reece. I'm done trying to make you love me. I'm done trying to make you see how much I love you." She shook her head. "I'm just done. I thought I could do this but apparently, I'm not willing to keep playing the fool forever. You know, I've put up with so much and I'm not going to anymore. You, for not being willing to take a chance on love and Nolan for slamming me against a wall just recently." She quickly walked out of the bedroom.

He followed her, caught her in the kitchen, and took her arm in his hand.

"When the hell did that happen?"

"It doesn't matter, does it? Preston and Deidra got there before he could do anything more to me."

"Did you tell Sam?"

"No—"

"Why the fuck not?"

"Because it would just piss Nolan off even more. Even if he was arrested, once he got out, he'd be back. I'm done with both of you."

"Your hair is wet," he said and wondered if he could have said anything more stupid.

"I don't care. You know, I had hopes that since we didn't just have a one-night stand, this would amount to something even though you told me it wouldn't." She pointed at him. "You are a coward, Reece Maddox. A fucking coward."

"I told you—"

"Yep, you did. Over and over, but you kept coming around, didn't you? According to what Preston told Deidra, you never do that. It really was just sex for you."

"Why else?" he said through clenched teeth and when she gasped, he felt like an ass.

"Glad we got that settled. I'm sure the next woman you see for sex will be happy because even though you're a coward, you're damn good in bed. Have a nice lonely life."

Rissa pulled her coat on, opened the door, walked out, and slammed it behind her.

"Son of a bitch," Reece roared.

****

Rissa climbed into her SUV then tore down the driveway. It would be a cold day in hell before he saw her break down. She'd never let him see her crying again. The first tear fell by the time she reached the end of the driveway. She had to stop several times along the road to wipe tears from her eyes, but she finally reached the parking lot at the diner. After pulling around to the back, she got out then ran up the stairs to her apartment. Opening the door, she stepped inside, slammed it behind her then leaned against it and slid to the floor. *Damn you, Reece Maddox!*

Ripley moved onto her lap, curled into a ball, and started purring. She ran her hand over the cat's soft fur and leaned her head back against the door as tears rolled down her cheeks.

"I knew it, Rip. I knew he'd break my heart."

She gently pushed Ripley off her lap and pushed to her feet. After locking the door, she took her coat off, hung it on the coat rack, and headed for the bathroom to blow dry her still-damp hair. She had given no thought to Nolan being around. It was close to three in the morning though, so he was probably sleeping. He was still in Clifton even though she'd told him it was over. After getting her hair dry, she undressed and crawled under the blankets. She pulled them up to her chin, closed her eyes, prayed for sleep, and hoped she never saw Reece Maddox again in this lifetime.

At seven, she entered the diner, waved at people, and made her way to the kitchen. Her aunt stopped what she was doing and looked at her.

"You look like hell," Connie said.

"Thanks, love you too." Rissa took her coat off and hung it on a peg, then removed an apron and pulled it on.

"You're not scheduled to work. Deidra said she was coming in."

"Yeah, well, I thought I'd have something better to do today but turns out I don't."

Connie walked to her and put her arm around her.

"Are you all right?"

"No, but I will be. Please, just let me work. I'll think too much if I don't."

"Of course. We're busy, so get out there," Connie said with a wink. "You might want to let Deidra know."

"Thank you, I will," Rissa said and tried to smile but her chin quivered, so she picked up a pad along with a pen then walked out to the patrons. She was running on no sleep, but she couldn't sit in that apartment because all she'd do was think. It was better to simply get on with her life.

By late March, she was sure she was getting to the point where she didn't cry as much. She hadn't seen Reece since the night she had left his home. He never came into the diner when she was there. It was as if he knew when she would be, and he avoided her. It was probably best because she'd no doubt, fall at his feet and beg him to take her home with him. God! She was pitiful.

As she sat on the stool in the kitchen, she waited while her uncle made her a burger. She needed a break since her feet were killing her. It had been non-stop all day. Looking up at the clock, she sighed with relief when she noticed she had fifteen minutes left on her shift.

"Quit watching the clock," Lanie said as she entered the kitchen removing her coat. After she hung it up, she lifted an apron off the hook and pulled it over her head.

"Aren't you early?"

"Yep, an hour. Trent is working on the barn and I didn't have anything to do."

"Well, since you're early, I'm leaving." Rissa hopped down from the stool. "I'll take my burger to go, Uncle Owen."

"You got it, kiddo," he said with a wink.

"Are you doing all right?" Lanie asked her.

"Yes. I don't fall apart as often."

"Rissa, I wish it had turned out different for you."

"Me too, but I knew what I was getting into with him. I had to take a chance." She pulled her apron off over her head and hung it up.

"I'm going out to fill coffee cups. I'll talk to you later." Lanie hugged her then disappeared from the kitchen.

"You just wait until I'm done here, and I'll walk you up." Owen waved the spatula at her.

"All right." She was getting so tired of people having to *walk her up* because no one knew where Nolan was. No one had seen him for a long while. Of course, that didn't mean he wasn't around.

A few minutes later, she unlocked her door, entered, and waved at her uncle as he stood at the bottom of the steps. After she locked the door behind her, she headed for the kitchen to eat her burger and prepare for a boring Saturday night.

As she sat at the table, she picked up her cellphone and called her cousin. She just wanted to talk to someone, and with Lanie working at the diner, and Deidra working on her illustrations, Sloane was the next best thing. She scrolled through her contacts, found her number, pushed *Call,* and waited for her cousin to answer.

"Hey, Rissa," Sloane said when she answered.

"How's my favorite cousin?"

"I'm doing fine. How are you?"

"I've been better, but that's a long story. When are you coming to Montana? You said after the first of the year. We're three months in already."

"Well, actually, I think I'll be there soon."

"Really? That's great," Rissa said and meant it. She loved her cousin. Sloane was like another sister to all of them.

"Yes. I hate it here now. I mean, I love Albuquerque, but I don't know what to do. Do you know what I mean?"

"I do. Did the bakery sell?"

"Yes, and the house. Doug kept his word. I got seventy-five percent of the money from that and half of what the bakery sold for. I'm just so angry that I let it go though."

"I know. You loved having that place. Come up here, and you can stay with me. I have a nice two-bedroom apartment. I'd love to share it with you."

"I'd love that. I just want to get as far away from Doug as I can."

"I get that," Rissa cleared her throat.

"Are you all right, Rissa?"

"No, but I will be. Stupid me, I fell in love with a man who doesn't love me. I thought I could handle being with him when I knew he had no desire to settle down but there I go thinking."

"Oh, I'm so sorry. Men are such dicks at times. Well, when I come up there, we can be miserable together."

Rissa laughed. "Sounds good. I'll let you go. I just wanted to say hi and tell you that we all miss you. Please let me know when you're coming up."

"I will. It will probably be before the end of this month, but I'll let you know for sure. Love you," Sloane said.

"Love you back." Rissa hit *End* on her phone then placed it on the table and continued to eat her burger. She couldn't wait to see her cousin. Maybe with Sloane living here with her, it would keep her mind off Reece. She snorted. *Yeah, right.*

****

Driving into town, Reece pulled into the parking lot of the Feed Store, parked the truck, and stepped out. When he entered the store, people inside waved or called out to him. He gave them all a wave, walked to the counter, and placed his order. After it was loaded, he climbed into his truck, then drove out of the parking lot and headed down Main Street. It had been a beautiful day, and now the sun was beginning to set, turning the sky blue, pink, and yellow.

As he drove down the street, he saw McCabe heading for the parking lot of the diner. Reece slammed on the brakes, pulled into a lot, turned around, and headed for the diner's lot. He pulled his truck in, threw it in Park, took his hat off, tossed it onto the seat, and stepped out.

"Hey," he yelled.

McCabe stopped in mid-stride, turned around then grinned. "Back for more, cowboy?"

Reece didn't stop his momentum as he stalked toward him. McCabe swirled around to give him a roundhouse kick, but Reece was ready this time. He grabbed McCabe's leg and held it, making him bounce on one foot to keep his balance.

"This time, I'm more than ready," Reece said through clenched teeth, then he drew his fist back and hit McCabe in the nose.

McCabe tried to pull his leg away, but with Reece holding onto it, he couldn't get his leg

200

loose so he hit Reece on the chin, making him let go. Only as Reece stumbled back, he grabbed Nolan by the shirt and punched him again.

"Let go of me," McCabe said through gritted teeth.

"Hell, no." Reece punched him again, making McCabe's head snap back, and blood pour from his nose.

"Is this the only way you can beat me?" McCabe spat blood out as it dripped into his mouth.

"Surprise attack? Sound familiar?" Reece shoved him away from him, and Nolan stumbled back then gained his footing.

McCabe swiped his sleeve across his nose, looked at it, then grinned at Reece.

"You shouldn't have let go of me because now, I'm going to finish this." He took a step toward him.

Reece waited, and when McCabe got close enough, he threw a punch, hitting him square on the chin, making Nolan land on his ass.

"Get up! You fucking pussy. Get the fuck up," Reece yelled and noticed that a crowd had gathered around them.

McCabe got to his feet again, took a stance, and stared at him.

"I have no idea what she sees in you, Maddox."

"Maybe because I'm more of a man than you are. You just like to bully her. If you ever put your hands on her again, I'll shoot you. She deserves a hell of a better man than you in her life."

"Oh yeah, who, Maddox? You? She doesn't want *you*," McCabe shouted, and as much as he hated to admit it, the bastard was right. Rissa didn't want him anymore and it hurt. It hurt like hell.

"Well, she sure as shit doesn't want you, McCabe. The difference is, I would never torment her like you do."

They circled each other.

"It's time to stop talking. Come on, let's do this." McCabe made another move toward him.

Reece moved fast and grabbed the front of his shirt again and hit him several times in the face until he fell to the ground and didn't get up. Reece leaned over him, put his hand on his shoulder, and raised his fist to hit him again.

"Reece!"

He turned around to see Sam jogging through the parking lot and pushing through the crowd. Sam stopped beside him and looked down at McCabe, then he squatted and checked for a pulse.

"He's not dead. He just can't take a punch," Reece said as he shook his hand to alleviate the pain from his swollen knuckles.

Sam straightened up. "Did you start this?"

"I did. I saw him when I was driving down Main Street. I told you payback was a bitch, Sam."

"Holy hell, Reece. You could lose your job over this," Sam said in a low tone of voice.

Reece rolled his shoulders, blew out a breath, and looked down at McCabe.

"I know, but I had to do this, Sam. This son of a bitch attacked me. He put me in the hospital. I owed him."

"I know—" Sam stopped when McCabe moaned, sat up, and looked up at him.

"Sheriff, he attacked me. Took me completely off guard. I want to press charges."

Reece glanced at Sam, then back to McCabe.

"Just like you did to me in Dewey's parking lot."

"I did no such thing."

Reece was about to say something when he saw Sam pull his handcuffs from his utility belt. Sam glanced at the crowd.

"Brody? Come here and cuff McCabe." Reece grinned until Sam turned to him. "Hands behind your back, Reece. You're under arrest for disorderly conduct."

"Are you fucking serious, Sam?"

"Do I look like I'm kidding? Both of you are going in."

"We're friends, Sam."

"And I'm also the sheriff. I can't let this go. There are way too many witnesses. I just hope to hell you don't lose your job over this little stunt of yours."

"Son of a bitch," Reece muttered but turned his back to Sam and put his hands behind him. He felt the cuffs go on then Sam took his arm and led him across the street behind Brody with McCabe and listened as Sam read him his rights.

Once inside the Sheriff's department, Reece looked over to see Betty Lou Harper behind the counter. She looked at him and shook her head in what had to be disgust. Yeah, he was rather disgusted with himself too. He couldn't believe it when Sam opened a cell door, removed the handcuffs, and motioned for him to go inside.

He took a deep breath and entered the cell then took a seat on the cot. He saw Brody put McCabe in the one next to him.

"How long am I in here for, Sam?"

"Could be up to ten days—"

Reece shot to his feet. "I can't stay here for ten days. I have a job to get to."

"If you have one, you mean. If Dave finds out, you're shit out of luck."

"Damn it to hell," he muttered and took a seat on the cot again.

"Yeah, and I'm pressing charges, Maddox," McCabe said.

"You need to shut the fuck up. You're in just as deep as he is. We all know it was you who attacked him in Dewey's parking lot. I think this ass-kicking you just took was justified, but I don't make the law, so sit the fuck down," Sam snapped.

Reece leaned his head back against the wall and knew he'd fucked up big time. Damn McCabe wasn't worth this and certainly not worth losing his job over.

"I'll want to press charges too, Sam. By the way, did you ever get to look at the video from Dewey's cameras?" Reece knew as well as Sam did that those cameras had never worked. Dewey just had them up to deter people from fighting in the parking lots.

"Cameras?" McCabe asked and Reece saw him swallow hard.

"I'm waiting to get them from Dewey," Sam said, playing along.

"Okay. Okay. I won't press charges. Can we just drop all of this? I'll leave this town and you'll never see me again. Isn't there a fine I can pay?" McCabe asked Sam.

Reece watched as Sam leaned against the wall, folded his arms, and stared at McCabe then he glanced at Brody, who stood leaning against the wall with his thumbs hooked on his utility belt. Both men looked intimidating as hell.

"I suppose I could have you both pay fines. You, McCabe, are to get out of my town and never come back. Don't even think of telling Reece's boss about this either," Sam said.

"I don't even know where he works. I promise I'll get out of town."

"And never contact Rissa again either," Reece said.

"I won't. You're welcome to her." McCabe looked at Sam. "Come on, Sheriff. I'll leave as soon as you let me out of here."

Sam blew out a breath. "I should keep both your asses in here for at least the night, but I'm tired of this shit with you two. It ends now. We clear?"

"Yeah, Sam," Reece said as he pushed to his feet. "Got it."

"Yes, sir," McCabe said as he did the same.

"Betty Lou, get their fines, please. One hundred dollars each then Brody, you can let them out. I'm going home to my wife."

Sam pushed off the wall, walked down the hallway, and out the back door. Brody unlocked the cell doors and nodded for them to go to the lobby to pay their fines. Reece stopped beside him.

"Thanks, Brody."

"I hope it works out for you, Reece. You're crazy if you let that woman go. I know, I've been there."

"I know." Reece slapped him on the shoulder then walked to the lobby and stood behind McCabe as he paid his fine, then he paid his.

"Your mama would be ashamed of you, Reece Maddox," Betty Lou said with a tsk and a shake of her head.

"Yes, ma'am." He ran his hand around the back of his neck and felt like he was a kid again being reprimanded by the high school principal.

After Reece paid his fine, he walked out of the building and watched McCabe walk down the street, get into his car, and drive off. He hoped he never saw him again in this lifetime. He looked toward the diner and to the windows above it, wondering if Rissa was there.

Taking a deep breath, he walked down the steps, crossed the street, and headed back to his truck. He opened the door and was about to climb in when he grabbed his hat, put it on then shoved the door closed and headed for the metal steps leading to Rissa's apartment. At the bottom, he looked up and tried to get his feet to move.

"She's right. You're a fucking coward, Maddox."

Huffing out a breath, he started to climb the steps, but when he stood in front of the door, he just couldn't bring himself to knock.

"Grow some damn balls, Maddox," he chastised himself.

He raised his hand and knocked on the door. He heard the locks turn then the door opened and there she stood. The woman who owned his heart.

"Can I come in?"

"Is this a booty call?"

Reece tipped his head down to hide a grin then raised it and looked at her.

"Not unless you want it to be." He lifted one arm and put his hand on the doorjamb above her head.

"I don't. What do you want?"

"Can I come in?" he repeated.

Rissa shrugged and opened the door wider for him to enter. He strode past her and inhaled her strawberry bubble bath. The door slammed behind him and he turned to look at her. She leaned back against the door, folded her arms, and stared at him. It took all his willpower not to grab her and pull her close.

"McCabe won't be bothering you anymore," he said.

"Why not?"

"Because I just beat the hell out of him, and after throwing us both in jail, Sam made him leave town." He flexed his sore hand.

"You were in jail?"

"Yep, both of us for fighting. Sam let us off with fines but made McCabe leave town and he promised never to bother you again."

Rissa straightened up. "Oh, is that why you came by? Well, thank you. I'm happy he's gone." She reached for the doorknob.

"No. That's not the only reason. I did want to tell you he was gone though."

"Then what else, Reece?"

"I wanted to tell you that..." Reece took a deep breath. "I love you."

Rissa's mouth dropped open, but then she snapped it shut. She blinked her eyes as if to wake up from a dream. Had she heard him right?

"What?" she whispered.

Reece reached her in two steps and cupped her face in his hands. "I said, I love you. I've fought it long enough."

"But—" His lips stopped her from saying more. When his tongue tangled with hers, she moaned. She pulled her lips from his. "Reece."

"I do love you, Darissa Gates. So much it scares the living hell out of me."

He took her hand, led her to the sofa, and motioned for her to take a seat.

She pulled her hand away from his. "Let me get this straight," she said folding her arms across her chest. "After telling me over and over that you will never fall in love with me or any other woman, you will never settle down, and that I don't have a right to know what's going on in your life or express a feeling over it, you now decide that you love me?"

"Yes," Reece said with a shrug.

"And I'm supposed to just believe that?"

"You said you love me."

"And I do...I'm not really sure why sometimes, but I do," Rissa said shaking her head. "But I'm not very sure right now if you deserve it."

"Oh my God, really," Reece took a step forward but she continued to glare at him. She wanted to throw her arms around his neck and smother him in kisses but she also wanted him to feel some of the uncertainty she'd felt for the past several weeks.

"Rissa, I probably don't deserve you at all," Reece said with a scowl. "I'll probably never deserve you but I realize now the reason you've been in my thoughts almost constantly since Helena was because you are *the* one."

"Well, I guess when you put it that way," she said, dropping her arms and looking at the floor to hide her grin. "I might have some conditions though, and you have to be sure about this."

"I've never been so sure of anything in my life, but..." He took hold of her arms and pulled her close.

"But?" Did she really want to hear what he was going to say? Anytime a *but* was added, it was rarely good news.

"I can't give up my job, Rissa. I've worked too hard to get where I am."

"Quit your job?" She was *not* expecting that.

"Yes. I won't, so if that's a problem, we'll have to work through it in some way."

"Reece, I would never ask you to quit your job. I know it's dangerous, but I also know you love it. Besides, your wearing that gun and badge is sexy to me." She pulled her arms free and hugged him.

Reece laughed. "Good. I won't take as many field cases—"

"Yes, you will. I don't want you to change anything you do. We'll be fine."

"We will, Rissa, because I know we will work through any problems we have. I'm not going to end up like my parents. You are the only woman I want for the rest of my life. I've been so miserable without you. I know that I never want to be without you again. You are my life."

"Do you—" She cleared her throat. "Are you saying you might want to get married? And have kids?"

"Yes, to both, but let me have you to myself for a little while longer. Okay?"

Rissa squealed and jumped into his arms, then kissed his lips. He took over and deepened it. He pulled her to the sofa and pushed her to her back then leaned over her and lifted his lips from hers.

"I'm not going to lie, Rissa, I'm scared. I don't want to lose you. Ever. But if you did want to go, I'd let you. So, tell me your conditions."

She laughed. "Well, I'll never want to go. I love you so much and I've worked too hard to get you to realize you love me. I think I fell for you that first night in the hotel. So, condition one is that the only way this relationship ends is if you end it because I won't. Ever. I love you so much, Reece. I hated seeing a future without you in it. Meeting you that night in Helena was fate to me."

"That was a hot night, wasn't it? No reason why there can't be more."

"Well, that's another condition. Although there already have been, you will make sure our nights, and days, are always that hot."

"Absolutely, your conditions aren't very difficult," Reece said with a grin. "Any more?"

"One more...believe it when I say I'm so happy I found my cowboy," she whispered as she looked into his gorgeous eyes.

"Not as happy as he is, baby." He pressed his lips to hers. "Rissa, I've never been in love. I never wanted to fall for anyone because I didn't want to end up like my parents but I love you so much, and I know I'll love you for the rest of my life. You stole my heart and I don't want it back. All I want is you and your love."

"You have it, Reece. You always will. You know, I believe we'll be just as much in love when we're ninety as we are now."

"More because I'll love you even more every day."

"Well, then you won't have any trouble meeting my conditions."

Rissa hoped if she was dreaming, she never woke up. She wanted this one dream to go on for the rest of her life. A long life with her cowboy.

Epilogue

It looked like winter was finally winding down. Although it was still chilly, Reece thought, as he and Shiloh followed behind Rissa and the horse she was riding. Just as Preston had done for Deidra, Reece had given Rissa a horse of her own. He knew how much she loved them and always wanted one of her own. He grinned as he thought back to taking her out to the barn as a surprise.

"Can I pick any horse to ride?" she had asked him.

"You can ride me," he said as he pulled her to him and took her lips in a deep kiss.

"I did this morning, but I'll happily do it again later, cowboy."

"Okay. As far as riding any horse, no. Come here. I'll show you which one you can ride." He took her hand in his, led her down the aisle of the barn, and stopped at a stall. "This one."

Rissa gasped when she looked at the beautiful chestnut horse with a black mane and tail. "Oh, my. What a beautiful horse."

Reece put his arms around her from behind and kissed her neck. "She's all yours."

She turned in his arms. "What?"

"She's yours. I bought her for you."

"Are you serious?" She blinked her eyes quickly.

"Hell, I didn't buy her for you to make you cry. I know how much you love horses, and you should have your own."

"She had to be expensive, Reece."

"I can afford it. Granted, I don't have as much money as Preston, but I do all right. Do you like her?" He jerked his chin at the horse.

Rissa threw her arms around him. "I love her, and I love you."

"I can never hear that enough, darlin'."

"Where did you get her?"

"From Holt. I remembered you saying you loved Morgans. She's five years old. Her name is Wildest Dreams, but you can name her whatever you want. I had him bring the horse over when we were in town earlier."

"Very sneaky. I love her name, so I won't change it. It seems to fit with us, because never in my wildest dreams did I think you'd ever love me."

"And I never thought I'd fall in love, so yeah, it does fit. Come on, let's get her saddled and we'll go for a ride."

"I'd love that."

"I have a saddle and tack for you too."

"You bought me a saddle?"

"Actually, I had one made for you. Noah Conway is one hell of a saddler. Luckily, he had one started for a customer, but they changed their mind and wanted a lighter color."

Reece led her to the tack room and stopped by a dark leather saddle sitting on a rail. He watched as she ran her hand over the soft leather. She lifted one of the fender straps and he knew she'd see *Conway Saddles* stitched on it. He folded his arms and waited until she walked around the back of the saddle. She looked at him then to the cantle.

"It has my name on a silver plate, in cursive. How does he do that?"

"He's damn good. His saddles sell across the country. Do you like it?"

"It's beautiful," she said in a choked voice.

Now as they rode in the north pasture, he couldn't stop looking at her. Why he'd been afraid to fall in love was something he'd never understand. Oh, sure, the emotion could be scary, but with this special woman in his life, he was going to have a good life ahead of him. He loved her more than he thought it possible to love anyone. Yeah, he took some ribbing from his friends, but he laughed it off. They were glad he was happy, and so was he. Even Cord was happy for him. He just wished Cord would find someone one day. He deserved to be happy too.

She smiled at him and it made him happy to see that smile aimed at him. God! He loved her so much. He reached over, took the reins in his hand to stop her horse, and looked at her.

"What is it?"

Now or never, Maddox. Now or never. After taking a deep breath, he dismounted, dropped the reins on the ground, and walked around Shiloh. Looking up at the love of his life, he suddenly panicked. What if she said no? Mentally shaking his head, he knew she wouldn't. She wanted to get married. He reached up and pulled her out of the saddle and set her feet on the ground.

"Darissa Gates, I love you more than I ever thought it possible to love someone. I want to spend my life with you, have children with you, and die in your arms." He dropped to one knee.

Rissa put her mitten-covered hands over her mouth, and as he looked at her, a tear rolled down her cheek.

Reaching into the pocket of his jacket, he removed the black velvet box he'd tucked there, opened it to show her a two-carat emerald cut diamond, and took her hand in his. "Rissa, will you marry me?"

"Yes! Of course, yes," she shouted as more tears rolled down her face.

He grinned up at her, removed her mitten, took the ring from the box, and slipped it on her finger then kissed her knuckles. He got to his feet just in time to catch her as she threw herself at him. He cupped her face in his gloved hands, pressed his lips to hers, and kissed her like his life depended on it. When he raised his head, he knew he had tears in his eyes but he didn't care. He was happy, happier than he'd ever been before. She loved him, heart and soul, and for that, he was eternally grateful. She smiled as she held her hand out in front of her and stared at the ring on her finger as tears rolled down her face.

"I don't want to put my mitten back on," Rissa said as she continued to stare at the ring. "It's so beautiful. Look how it catches the light."

He grinned as he watched her hold her hand up high to let the rays of the sun make the ring sparkle.

"Life will never be boring with you," he said with a grin.

Rissa laughed. "Let's hope not. I will never regret that night in Helena."

"Me neither, sweetheart. I lost my heart to you that night and you will forever hold it."

When she blinked more tears from her eyes, Reece pulled her into his arms, kissed her forehead, and thanked God for her, and for letting him see that love wasn't so scary after all.

The End

About the Author

Susan was born and raised in Cumberland, MD. She moved to Tennessee in 1996 with her husband and they now live in a small town outside of Nashville, along with their two rescued dogs. Although writing for years, it was in 2014 that she decided to submit to publishers and she chose Secret Cravings Publishing. When SCP closed their doors, Susan decided to publish on her own. She is a huge Nashville Predators hockey fan. She also enjoys fishing, taking drives down back roads, and visiting Gatlinburg, TN, her family in Pittsburgh, PA and her hometown. Although Susan's books are a series, each book can be read as standalone books. Each book will end with a HEA and a new story beginning in the next one. She would love to hear from her readers and promises to try to respond to all.

She would also appreciate reviews if you've read her books.

You can visit her Facebook page and website by the links below.

https://www.facebook.com/skdromanceauth or

www.susanfisherdavisauthor.weebly.com
susan@susanfisherdavisauthor.com